GHOUL SUMMER

ALSO BY TRACY BADUA

Freddie vs. the Family Curse

The Takeout

Thea and the Mischief Makers

The Cookie Crumbles (with Alechia Dow)

Their Just Desserts (with Alechia Dow)

GHOUL SUMMER

TRACY BADUA

STORYTIDE
An Imprint of HarperCollins*Publishers*

HarperCollins Children's Books, a division of HarperCollins Publishers,
195 Broadway, New York, NY 10007

HarperCollins Publishers, Macken House, 39/40 Mayor Street Upper,
Dublin 1, D01 C9W8, Ireland

Storytide is an imprint of HarperCollins Publishers.

Ghoul Summer
Copyright © 2025 by Tracy Badua
All rights reserved. Manufactured in Harrisonburg, VA,
United States of America.
No part of this book may be used or reproduced in any manner whatsoever without written permission except in the case of brief quotations embodied in critical articles and reviews. Without limiting the exclusive rights of any author, contributor, or the publisher of this publication, any unauthorized use of this publication to train generative artificial intelligence (AI) technologies is expressly prohibited. HarperCollins also exercises their rights under Article 4(3) of the Digital Single Market Directive 2019/790 and expressly reserves this publication from the text and data mining exception.
harpercollins.com
Library of Congress Control Number: 2025935139
ISBN 978-0-06-334705-2
Typography by Andrea Vandergrift
25 26 27 28 29 LBC 5 4 3 2 1
FIRST EDITION

For those I have the privilege of watching grow up and old

1

Summer at a luxury beachfront house with its own hot tub and high-tech entertainment system? I never thought I'd say this, but count me out.

Too bad no one listens to me, though.

The salty ocean air streams into the minivan from Mom's open window. From the front seats, she and Dad point out all the boring stuff—the long boardwalk for morning strolls, the cute but weathered theater and stores on Main Street, limited parking—while my little brother, Leo, stays glued to one of the dozen graphic novels he brought along for the car ride. I envy him. I can't even read a candy bar wrapper in the car without getting sick. So I've just spent this three-hour drive to Sunnyside trying to nap and tune out my parents' not-so-subtle hints at how wonderful they expect this summer to be.

"A toy shop, Barnaby, look! Such cute stuffed animals!" Mom says, a dark brown arm jutting out of the window and pointing into the distance. Her nails are festive, tropical red. Unlike me, she's fully adopted the vacation mindset, even though we're here more for business than fun.

I can't suppress the groan. "Mom, a toy shop might have been a draw for me when I was Leo's age, but I'm twelve."

"You're never too old for a cute stuffie," Mom counters.

Instead of the action-packed summer I'd planned with my friends at home, this will be three weeks of helping Grandpa pack up his house so he can move in with us. No number of stuffed animals can make up for that.

Before we left home, Mom had a whole talk with me about "attitude." So I unclench my jaw enough to at least utter a "Great."

"Oh dear, it looks like they're finally tearing down the Grand Seabird," Mom says, pointing ahead.

I follow her gaze to the ragged skyline. A temporary construction fence lined with *Danger* and *Keep Out* signs surrounds a stately, late-1800s resort.

"About time. I don't think I've ever seen that place open," I say. We've visited Sunnyside annually for as long as I can remember, more frequently last year when Grandma got sick. And at none of those times did I ever see any lights flickering in the windows of the Not-So-Grand Seabird.

Mom sighs wistfully. "What a shame. It's such a beautiful place."

I shrug. "Time to make room for the new, I guess."

Mom shakes her head like I've missed the point of whatever she said. Then the GPS app on Dad's phone announces that our destination is just ahead.

Our minivan pulls into the narrow concrete driveway of a two-story, vivid blue house with pristine white trim. A balcony hangs over the garage, and bronze lanterns flank the stained-glass-windowed door. A seagull-shaped weather vane sits atop the gray-shingled roof.

"Warner Place." Dad whistles. "Wow, it's better than the pictures in the rental listing."

"I can't believe we got it at such a low price," Mom says.

"Well, it technically has only two bedrooms and an office, but the owner, Mr. Morgan, recently cleared out the attic and said we could use it too. He said we'd likely be some of the last guests in this place. He's waiting for some permits to build something else here. It's why they let us bring Pao even though almost every rental has a no-pets policy." Dad reaches over to pet the head of our white Maltese, who's snoozing in Mom's lap.

"I call that hammock on the balcony!" Leo blurts out. "Perfect reading spot."

A quiet, screen-free hobby? The nine-year-old wins the competition for Best Kid in our family, hands down.

I lean forward to get a better look. All right, I'll admit it doesn't look terrible. It looks *welcoming*, even.

But I refuse to let go of how angry I am that Mom and Dad sprang the trip on us. My summer with Cru and Morris was going to be epic, but now—goodbye, afternoon-long gaming hangouts, horror flick marathons, and extra scoops of ice cream from Cru's cousin at Fifteen Flavors of Frozen Fun.

This place better have excellent Wi-Fi.

"It's fine, I guess."

"A five-star review, coming from you," Dad says with a wink.

I don't scowl, which I think is a polite enough response. To Dad's credit, he offered me his debit card so I could buy the more portable version of *Warricane Five*. I'd saved up all my birthday money and allowance to buy *the game* of the year on our desktop computer at home, only to have this trip thrown at me last minute. My parents wouldn't allow me to stay home alone for the three weeks, like I begged. This game will at least let me try to stay connected to Cru and Morris.

Ten minutes later, I haul my suitcase and a bag of groceries up the small flight of wooden stairs to the front door. Dad is on the phone with Mr. Morgan, assuring him everything is perfect, and Mom is already testing out the Wi-Fi speed on her work laptop. I deposit the groceries just inside the door, under a framed painting of a sailboat. Mom insisted we bring a billion bags of garlic shrimp chips because they don't sell them in this town. We made room for garlic shrimp chips but not our desktop computer? Unfair, if you ask me (which no one did).

As I'm about to head upstairs with my suitcase, Mom calls out, "Everything from the trunk, Barnaby, please."

I sigh, drop my suitcase, then go to retrieve more bags from the back of the van. That way, no one can get on my case for having a bad attitude or not being a team player. I just want to get through this three-week speed bump in my summer plans as quickly and argument-free as possible. No extra sightseeing, no trying to make new friends I'll never see again, no doing anything that could lengthen our stay here.

I pass Leo on the way down. The kid is trying to finish his graphic novel, carry his duffel bag, and navigate the stairs all at once.

Something cold slips past the back of my neck then, like a short blast of air conditioning when you walk past a freezing store in the middle of summer. It's not from inside the house. I glance up, expecting a rustling palm tree or, worse, the shadow of a seagull ready to poop on me. There's nothing but a clear, sunny sky.

"Did you feel that?" I ask my brother.

He doesn't even glance up. "Feel what?"

"Never mind." I quicken my pace and grab three grocery bags from the minivan. I spot what I think is a puddle underneath and squat to investigate. But it's not a puddle; it's a single red brick.

Warner 1898

This brick must have been part of the original road before they paved everything over with the smooth concrete that lines the paths to the neighboring houses. I take the stairs to the house two at a time and sidle past Leo, who has stopped short of the door to finish his page.

When I step inside, my leather flip-flops land with a crunch. I glance down at the dark, polished wood floor to find a sea of shrimp chips, the huge bag I'd left here completely torn open.

A gasp draws my attention. "Barnaby, what did you do?"

I know that tone. Mom's upset, but I can't imagine why. I'm *helping*, aren't I?

"I didn't do anything. I just brought the bags up like you asked."

Ahead, Mom's face is pinched, and somehow Pao's furry expression matches hers. Dad is still on the phone somewhere deeper in the house, and Leo hasn't made it past the door yet.

"Then what happened here?"

Mom sets down Pao, who, ever-obedient, stays at her feet. Our dog does peer up at me with something resembling sympathy, though. Or maybe she only wants a chip.

"I have no clue. Maybe the bag was already open? I set it down and went outside to get more groceries!"

Mom eyes the bags still hanging on my shoulders. That part of my story checks out. "I know you don't want to be here, Barnaby, but—"

"Come on, Mom. How could you think I'd take my anger out on a defenseless bag of delicious snacks?"

She shakes her head. "We'll talk about this later. I'm going to find a broom. You are cleaning this mess up."

She begins to walk away. Pao, who typically stays close on Mom's heels, instead pads toward the chip mess. She takes a tentative sniff, then gives me a suspicious look.

"Pao, don't you dare eat one," I warn. Who knows what a highly processed fried chip will do to her little digestive system?

To my horror, Pao's digestive system answers me. Before I can stop her, pee trickles onto the crushed chips and hardwood floor.

"Pao, no!" I shriek, and Mom comes running back. She takes one look at the mess, then adorable, innocent-looking Pao, then me.

"I'll find a mop too," Mom says, her voice tight.

I rub the back of my neck and sigh. "Yes, please, a mop too."

Mom stalks away, and Pao follows. I feel it again, that inexplicable wisp of coldness.

A cough sounds behind me. "Whoa, what happened here?"

Wonderful. Leo finished his book right in time to pester me for something I didn't do.

I hold my breath and tiptoe around the soggy chips. We just arrived, and I already can't wait to get home.

2

Once Mom hands me the broom and mop, I clean up the soggy snacks without any further chip crushing, pet accidents, or commentary from Leo. When I go to stow the cleaning supplies away, I get a good look at the inside of our home for the next few weeks.

Wide windows let in plenty of sunlight. The wood-paneled walls have been painted a cool, calming white, and seashell- or sailboat-themed decor adorns almost every free surface. Two big, comfortable-looking blue armchairs sit near a box window.

I tug open a door to a walk-in pantry that's nearly empty except for a few bottles of cleaning solution. It's cool and musty in here, and for a moment, I almost catch a hint of something sweet and citrusy. It's not the pine-scented cleaning solution. It almost smells like limes, as if someone is hand-squeezing them for a pie.

I shake my head to clear the sensation. The long drive must've gotten to me. The pantry shelves are bare of anything fresh and look like they have been for ages.

"What's in there?"

Leo's voice makes me jump. I tuck the broom and mop away next to a stack of buckets.

"Nothing."

"Have you seen the TV in the living room yet? It's awesome. The remote has a thousand buttons on it, and the speakers—"

"You didn't open the shrimp chip bag, did you?" I cut in as I shut the pantry door. "Because I could've sworn it was sealed when I brought it in."

Leo shakes his head, his straight bowl-ish cut swishing around as he moves. "You know I don't like to spoil my appetite."

I snort. More points for the perfect kid. Then there's me, who apparently can't even help bring in groceries right.

"Do you think Pao got into the bag?"

"She only eats her prescription kibble."

Pao, the perfect dog (even if she doesn't have the best bladder control), pushes me further down in the family rankings. No wonder Mom assumed I was the most likely to rip open a bag of chips and sprinkle them on the floor like a flower girl at a wedding.

I head back to my suitcase by the front door. A breeze floats down the staircase that leads to the second-floor bedrooms and office. Dad and Mom must already be up there, opening the windows to air the place out.

Behind me, Leo's duffel bag rustles as he hoists it up. He already claimed the hammock: no way I'm going to lose the battle for best bedroom. My legs spring into action, and I barrel up the stairs.

On the second level, I glance to my left. A four-poster bed takes up most of the space in the main bedroom, and Dad is already unpacking his toiletries.

To my right is a tiny office, with a simple wood-and-metal desk pushed up against a window and a ship in a bottle perched on a shelf nearby. Mom dumped her home office supplies on the floor. She's planning on working most mornings.

A few more steps down the hallway and I spot another room. This one is clean and cozy, with a plush blue rug on the floor and a flat-screen TV mounted on a pastel-blue wall. It might do.

I'm about to step in when I get the eerie sense that someone's watching me. I freeze. Leo isn't up the stairs yet—that's what happens when you pack half your weight's worth in graphic novels—and my parents haven't emerged from their bedroom. Pao isn't anywhere in sight. She's probably curled up on the bed in the other room, watching Mom hang up the fancier work-from-home shirts she brought.

Then, out of the corner of my eye, I spot a narrow spiral staircase at the far end of the hall. It's white and welcoming like the rest of this house. Taking one last peek to make sure Leo is far enough away to keep from claiming this too, I head up the stairs. My suitcase bangs against the metal railings as I ascend.

I emerge into a small but airy room, with low-sloped ceilings like I'm just underneath the roof. This must be the attic Dad mentioned.

I set down my suitcase. This room is more sparsely furnished than the rest of the house, with only a bed, some throw pillows, and a desk. There's a paper tag on the curtains like the decorator just bought them.

A thump and a creak from downstairs: Leo must have thrown down his duffel bag and claimed the blue bedroom. Good. I'm more likely to be left alone in this room on the top floor.

I stroll to one of the windows, the floorboards creaking beneath me, and am rewarded with a gorgeous view of the ocean. Cru and Morris would be so jealous. I wonder what level they are in *Warricane* now. We were supposed to play together as a team, but with me stuck here, their characters will gather more experience and level up by the day. Meanwhile, my character is going to languish with measly beginner stats for three weeks. It might be impossible to catch up. My annoyance surges again at the thought of how this trip managed to wreck my entire summer and probably my whole *Warricane* life.

I tug my phone out of my pocket to text my friends.

Cru immediately texts back. **A third-story room all to yourself? I'm still bunking with the twins!**

Then Morris: **Show us! Please? I'm stuck in Dad's office all day, staring at him on a conference call.**

I pull up my camera to take a picture. To get the clearest view, I slide open the window to move the dust-dotted glass out of the way, then step back. Billowy white curtains flit in the breeze. A seagull soars in the distance. The warm afternoon sun sparkles across the water.

Okay, so this summer may not be so awful after all. Not that I'd ever tell my parents I'm anywhere near happy with missing a huge chunk of summer with my friends.

I hold my camera steady, click, then go to inspect my work. My photo captures the vacation vibes perfectly.

But sitting on the windowsill is something that I hadn't expected in the frame. My breath catches in my throat.

There's a boy with short, wavy brown hair, wearing an oversize teal T-shirt and khaki shorts.

And he's glowering at me.

3

Silently, the boy hops off the windowsill and stalks toward me.

"Excuse me, this is *my* room," he says.

I hide my surprise with a frown of my own. If this kid thinks he's going to bully me out of here, he's wrong. He doesn't know that this year I successfully argued myself out of two detentions for being late to class.

"My family rented this house for the next three weeks. My dad signed a contract and everything," I say.

The boy rolls his eyes. "A contract doesn't change anything. This is still *my* room. You can't waltz in here and throw your junk all over the place."

"What junk?" I ask. The room is spotless. "I literally just arrived."

He glares at the suitcase I'd left on the landing. He stretches his fingers out, then curls them in to make fists.

The strained zipper pops open, and a T-shirt sleeve, a pair of underwear, and a phone charging cord spill out. I'd spent so long trying to cram every possible thing into that bag. At least I made it up the stairs before it gave way.

I stride over to my suitcase to cram my belongings back in. This random kid may not belong here, but I still don't want him getting a view of my Super Mario undies.

"Like I said," I grumble, "the owner, Mr. Morgan, rented this house to us for the next three weeks. My parents and my brother are unpacking, but I don't see the rest of your family here. So for all I know, you're the one who isn't supposed to be in this house, and we should probably call Mr. Morgan to get you kicked out."

"If I'm not supposed to be here, then why is my name carved into the wall?" He juts a thumb over to the windowsill. "Look behind that curtain on the left."

"So, what, you broke in and vandalized the place? You're not helping your case."

He rolls his eyes again, like I'm the one who's being annoying. "Just look! I'm Maxwell."

With a sigh, I shove down the top of my suitcase again, rezip it, then head over to the window and draw back the curtain. There, carved into the wall and painted over in thick white paint, is a name.

Maxwell Warner 1984

The confusion settles in like a fog, and I struggle to see through it. "Warner, like the brick out in the driveway."

"This house has been in my family for generations. My great-grandfather built it."

"It belongs to Mr. Morgan now, so you're probably not allowed to be here anymore."

The boy groans. "Don't even get me started on that dude. No one's ever bothered me in the attic before, but he keeps on finding fresh ways to ruin this place. I used to have the coolest *E.T.* poster over there." His eyes drift to a wall that now holds a decorative wooden steering wheel.

I look again at the carving and do the math. "But you can't be this Maxwell Warner person from 1984. Unless your dad or grandpa was named that too?"

"Wrong. My grandpa's Ellis, my dad is Gene. I was named after my mom's uncle."

"If that carving is yours, you'd be, like, fifty years old, but you're . . ."

He nods impatiently, like he's had this conversation a million times before. "I look eleven. I know. Because that's how old I was when I died and got stuck in this house, so you see why I can't let you take over this one space that's mine, right?"

I stagger back, my pulse booming in my ears. "Whoa, you're skipping a thousand steps here. I—I need some time to catch up."

"Catch up to what? That I'm dead?" He says it casually, like he's telling me his shoe size.

I nod. "I'm dreaming, aren't I?" I run through everything that brought me here—from the waffles for breakfast to the long drive to the ache of my muscles as I unloaded the car. "There's no way a regular day would be so boring and then suddenly . . . well, whatever this is."

"Hate to break it to you, but you're wide awake. And you're in my space," he says.

"I—I need to sit down." I fumble my way over to the bed, which creaks when I plop on top. And because this is further proof that this will indeed be the worst summer ever, I grab a seashell-printed throw pillow and scream into it.

Maxwell waits until I'm done to speak. "Wait, you're not terrified of me? Most people speed straight out of here."

I lower the pillow from my face. "I'm not 'most people,' then. Sure, I've never met a ghost before, so this is pretty weird, but ghosts and anything otherworldly don't really scare me. Back when my grandma was alive, she'd tell me about the spirits and creatures she'd seen in the Philippines and in her travels around the United States with Grandpa. She'd encountered a particularly mean ghost in the ladies' restroom of a Chicago restaurant. You don't seem like that. You just seem like an annoying kid."

He purses his lips. "I wasn't violently murdered or

anything, so I'm not one of those scary evil ghosts like the one in *Poltergeist*."

"Polter-what?"

This ghost has the audacity to rub his temples like I'm giving him a headache. I think my disorientation here is totally justified.

"I just mean I'm not here to hurt anyone. I want to be left alone. Past renters at least stayed downstairs and out of my way. Look, your family seems really nice—aside from those weird-smelling chips you hauled in here—but I'm going to need you gone so I can hang out in peace without any intruders around. Nothing personal."

I raise an eyebrow. "Um, that sounds totally personal, and those shrimp chips are delicious." My eyes widen with realization. "Wait, was that you? The ripped-open bag?"

He nods. "I had to get your attention somehow! Your parents were busy on their phones or with the dog."

"You got their attention all right, and I was blamed for it." I squeeze the seashell pillow to get some angry energy out.

"How about a compromise? Your family can stick around, but you stay out of the attic. You can bunk with that other boy."

My nose scrunches reactively. "Share a room with my little brother for three weeks? No thanks. I'm staying. We rented this house fair and square. If anyone should leave this room and this house, it's you. You've basically been living in—or, I guess, haunting—this place free of charge for decades."

Maxwell laughs. "I don't think you understand how being a ghost works."

"I don't think you understand how rent works. My mom's a lawyer, and she does housing stuff all the time," I exaggerate. She's a divorce lawyer, but divorced people have to deal with houses too, right? "You don't pay, you don't stay."

Maxwell's amusement fades, and his glower returns. "I'm asking you really nicely to leave," he says, his jaw tight, "or else."

I narrow my eyes. "That doesn't sound like nice asking to me. That sounds like a threat."

"I know I said I'm not out to hurt anyone, but I can make your time here very, very unpleasant. You don't want to get on my bad side."

I bark out a laugh. As if this trip could get more unpleasant at this point. My parents drag me hours away from home during what was supposed to be a fun summer with friends. Leo and Pao are cooperating, painting me as even more of the bad guy. And now I can't even wallow alone in peace because the one remaining bedroom is haunted?

I lift my chin. "Trust me, you don't want to get on mine

either. Give me an hour with reliable internet connection and I'll find a way to banish your butt out of here."

"You wouldn't," he says, taking another step toward me. He's practically in my face now. He's my height, and up close, I can tell his eyes must've been a greenish brown, his face a light peach.

I lift my chin higher and stare at him down the bridge of my flat nose. "Oh, I would. And I don't even want to be here."

"I guess this means war, then."

"I guess it does. You're going to regret ever going up against Barnaby Vargas."

His glower deepens, and I hear my suitcase snap back open with a loud pop. I whirl around. The zipper is completely busted, and my clothes are strewn everywhere. I dash over to at least snatch the Super Mario underwear that's now hanging on the staircase railing—seriously, of all the things on display for this ghost—and hurl it into the bag.

I spin back around, my fists clenched. "Gah, you are so annoying! You'd better not—"

The words fade into nothing. There's no use arguing. Maxwell is gone.

4

I grab my tablet and stomp downstairs, past Leo hanging up his clothes in the closet and Mom already at work in the office. I head for the small backyard patio to the side of the kitchen. Fresh air and a chat with my friends will clear my head.

I settle into a chair at the metal-and-glass table. The backyard is bordered by a white picket fence and potted plants so green I suspect they may be fake. In the yard next door, an elderly Black woman hums to herself as she fills a watering can. She doesn't see me yet, and I'd rather not announce myself. I'm having enough trouble with the first person I met here.

I angle my chair away, facing the ocean instead of her house. I feel instantly more relaxed being outside.

Cru answers after a few rings, and his face spreads

across my tablet screen. The picture freezes for a moment. I clench my jaw. The Wi-Fi is slow and glitchy, not at all as my parents promised.

A gaming headset tamps down part of Cru's poofy red curls. "Hey, Barn! Morris is coming over to play *Warricane*. You in?"

My chest squeezes. "No, not this time. This vacation house's Wi-Fi is terrible. I doubt it could handle even the blockiest graphics. I'll need to see if we can get it fixed first."

"You should've stayed home. You're missing out!"

Somehow, Cru stating the obvious makes me feel even worse. "Oh, I know. I kept trying to convince my parents it'd be fine. Just leave me with a bunch of frozen waffles."

Cru snorts a laugh. Then he leans close to his camera so that my screen is zeroed in on his face. "Um, your hair, bro—is there a hurricane happening or something?"

I blink. "What do you mean?"

"It's doing this weird thing on its own." He snorts again.

On its own? I tap on the tiny square that shows my camera view, and it enlarges to reveal Maxwell behind me, fluffing up my hair so it looks like devil horns.

"Quit it!" I snap at Maxwell.

Cru raises an eyebrow. "Who, me? Sorry, I didn't know"—the video freezes—"sensitive about your hair."

I whirl around. "No, you! Leave me alone!"

The ghost drops his hands and starts whistling in a display of innocence so obviously fake.

I angle back to the tablet. "Can't you see him?"

Cru squints. "See who? I thought you just wanted to gloat about that nice ocean breeze."

I drag a palm down my face. "I've gotta go."

After Cru hangs up, I lower my tablet to find Maxwell sitting across from me. His grin makes my blood boil.

"Can you not do that?"

"Do what?" More fake innocence.

"Mess with me like that! My friend couldn't see you. I looked totally weird to him."

"You know there's an easy solution to this," he says. "Leave."

"Right. *You* should leave."

He glowers. "No. You."

"No. You!" I yell right as a couple Rollerblades by. When they gasp, I throw out a "Sorry, talking to someone on Bluetooth," even putting a hand to my ear as if I actually have earbuds in. They roll away, peeking back to make sure I'm not following them.

"Great," I grumble. "I can't even have peace out here."

I grab my tablet and trudge inside, hoping Maxwell doesn't follow. If it were up to me, I *would* leave. I don't have any desire to spend the summer going toe-to-ghost-toe with him over a place I don't even want to be. But as my parents have told me a dozen times, my own summer plans are not, in fact, up to me.

Dad is in the kitchen, cutting up an apple, when I slide the glass door closed behind me. "Snack?"

I shake my head. "We should get a hotel. I don't want to be here."

Dad tilts his head. "Is something wrong?"

Now, if there's anything I've learned from television, it's that you can't come right out and say that you see ghosts or that aliens abducted you or that vampires exist. It catches people off guard, and they might react in awful ways, like locking you up. My dad is awesome at grilled cheese sandwiches, selecting movies we can all agree on, and cheering embarrassingly loudly any time our school makes us sing or dance. But I have seen him blow little things out of proportion, like when I put that teensy dent in the side of the van with my bike. I don't know what a vacation grounding would look like, but I'm not eager to find out.

"I don't like it here. There's no door on the attic room. The bed is lumpy. The vibe is all wrong."

Dad pauses his fruit cutting. "The vibe? Barnaby, we already paid for this place. I'm not going to lose our deposit and spend three times as much for a hotel because you don't like the vibe."

I try a different tack. "It also feels really unsafe. I

almost slipped and busted my head open on those spiral stairs!"

"Then you'll just have to slow down or, better yet, stay downstairs and spend time with your brother!" He shakes his head when I grimace at his suggestions. "Anyway, they wouldn't rent out this place if it wasn't safe. Every property goes through a bunch of certifications and inspections before they put it on the rental company website."

Too bad that rental company doesn't inspect for ghosts.

I'm failing at convincing Dad that we should leave. I have to be more direct.

"Can we stay at Grandpa's, then? I get this odd sense, like this place is"—I fix my eyes seriously on his—"haunted."

I hope for any hint that he's open to the idea of ghosts. He's heard Grandma's stories too, after all. She used to tell us about a headless monk ghost who haunted a bridge back in the Philippines. At least our fancy-vacation-rental ghost isn't that. But I don't see curiosity or even fear in Dad's eyes. I see impatience.

"There's no space at Grandpa's. It's small enough as it is, and he's already packed up his guest room. We'd have to cram onto the living room floor in between boxes for three weeks." He sets down his knife. "You know what I think? You're still mad at your mom and me for coming here this summer. But this is important."

I set my tablet down on the counter. "I'm not mad— well, I am, but this isn't that. I just don't want to stay here."

Something glimmers next to Dad. Maxwell appears, sitting on the kitchen counter, swinging his legs gleefully. Dad doesn't even sense that he's there. I hate that ghost.

"Please?" I add.

Dad shakes his head. "Barnaby, no. We're staying, and that's final. And I don't want to hear another word about hauntings. You know how overactive your brother's imagination gets."

"But, Dad, if there really is a ghost, then don't you think—"

"Stop. That's the end of this. If your brother overhears you and gets scared, he's sleeping in your room, not ours, got it?"

Maxwell stops swinging his legs. "You're doing a real bad job at convincing your dad to leave."

"Butt out!" I snap at him.

Dad crosses his arms. "Excuse me?"

"I— Sorry. I was—" I don't have a good explanation for this.

Maxwell laughs, then blinks out of sight. All the mischief, none of the consequences.

"Come on, Barnaby," Dad says, the anger leaching from his voice. "At least try to have a good time, okay? You've got everything here: your tablet, the beach, your family . . ."

"But not my friends. The Wi-Fi here is glitchy and awful. I can't even game with Cru and Morris."

"Then go out and make new friends. There are plenty of people on the beach if you wanted to put on your swim trunks. We're not going to Grandpa's until tomorrow anyway."

I groan, then choose an option that sidesteps Dad's suggestion of throwing myself at more Sunnyside residents. "I'll—I'll walk Pao. Maybe there's somewhere she can run around nearby."

"That's the spirit. You want to come introduce ourselves to our neighbor first? I thought I saw her outside. She might know a dog park around here."

I shake my head. "You know Pao doesn't like dog parks or, really, any other dogs. Not after that Chihuahua nipped at her leg."

"Maybe she'll like the park here," Dad suggests.

I grab the leash from where it hangs on the back of a chair. "We'll see." But I know Pao, and she's like me. We both prefer snacks instead of meals, enjoy plenty of couch time, and get nervous when Mom expresses a need for us to get haircuts. And neither of us has any desire to make new friends.

5

The boardwalk stretches a mile along the coast, leading from the run-down Grand Seabird, past rows of beach houses like ours, to the strip of mostly vacant storefronts. Pao trots happily down the concrete, the wind in her snowy-white fur. She's in a good mood.

My mood, on the other hand, dips every time I think about returning to Warner Place and seeing Maxwell. As Pao sniffs at a lamppost, I text Morris. He'll know what to do: He's the one who usually picks horror flicks for our movie marathons. He's probably watched a hundred ghost ones.

He, Cru, and I have been friends for ages. Teachers even started calling us the Three Musketeers, though I don't quite understand what our friend group has to do with the candy bar. We're on such a similar wavelength that I don't even have to give Morris background when I text him through the group thread we share with Cru.

Me: Best way to get rid of a ghost?

Morris answers right away. **Good or bad?**

I pause. Is Maxwell good? He doesn't seem outright evil, but he's definitely not Casper-friendly either.

Me: Annoying.

Morris: You can try burning sage, like they did in Midnight Monster 3. Ghosthunter Franz uses salt in her show.

As I consider those options, Cru jumps into the chat too.

Cru: Wait, you have a ghost? You can help solve their unfinished business!

I snort while typing.

Me: *I* don't have a ghost. There's a ghost pestering me. And unfinished business would mean spending more time with that ghost—no thanks.

Morris: That's awesome! Tell me everything later, Mom is getting on my case about screen time.

Cru: Warricane late tonight then? In the meantime, there's always good old-fashioned exorcisms!

I smile down at my phone. I knew I could count on them. Shooting off a quick thanks, I beckon Pao toward home so we can raid the cupboards for sage. A group of people on electric scooters zoom down the boardwalk at us, so we duck onto a palm-tree-lined side street and take a less busy way home. The sound of barks draws my attention. Across the street is a small fenced-in dog park. I peer at Pao, who has stopped and is staring at the dogs chasing each other in the free space. "Want to drop in?" I ask her.

Not that I expect a dog to answer. But I look for any sign of her wanting to go in—a step, a sniff, a tug, anything. She simply resumes walking in the direction of Warner Place, and I follow her.

The kitchen is empty when we return. Dad must be out introducing himself to more neighbors. He's probably halfway down the block by now. I did not inherit his golden retriever–like social sense.

Glass jars of spices pack the cabinet next to the stove. I rummage through them and grab the salt, but none of the other containers read *sage*. I open a drawer and find matches and old packets of red pepper flakes and the herb seasoning they give out at pizza places.

At first glance, this house looks magazine-ad generic. It has the right amount of gauzy white curtains and firm furniture for guests to feel invited in but not for too long. Yet, hidden in drawers and dusty corners of the place are artifacts of visitors past. I wonder how many families like mine have gathered in this kitchen with take-out pizza over the years. I wonder if that annoying ghost did.

I pick up the herb seasoning. Does this have sage in it? A cold feeling brushes my neck as I'm mulling over the ingredients. When I whirl around, Maxwell is perched on the kitchen counter. He looks comfortable, as if waiting for someone to take cookies out of the oven so he can grab one fresh off the sheet. Pao growls at him, then scurries behind me.

"Ready to leave?" he asks with a smirk. "I packed your bag for you. You should really buy some new shirts. Three of them have holes in the armpits."

I glower and slide an empty frying pan onto the stove. "Actually, I'm getting ready to kick you out. Do ghosts even have bags to pack?"

Maxwell's eyes slide to the spices. "What've you got there?"

"Just the stuff to send you flying out of here," I say. I rip open the spice packets and dump the dried herbs into the pan. With the flick of a match, I set the leaves on fire. They combust and release a small, thick cloud of smoke that scratches my throat and sends me coughing.

I pick up the pan and jut it at Maxwell. "Be gone, ghost!"

But instead of screeching and dissolving, Maxwell raises a slightly transparent eyebrow at me. "What—what are you doing?"

"I'm burning sage! Be gone, I said!"

Maxwell snickers. "Um, I think those packets are mostly oregano. Who puts sage on pizza?"

I practically growl as I fling the pan back on the stove and reach for the salt. Ghosthunter Franz is the best in the business—if Morris says she uses this, it must work.

I pour the salt directly into my hand. "Last chance, Maxwell. If you don't leave now, this is going to banish you far, far away, and I doubt it'll be pretty."

This time, fear flickers across Maxwell's face. "You—you don't scare me. Do your worst!"

"You leave me no choice. Be gone, ghost!" I chuck the salt at him. It rains down through his form and onto the kitchen counter.

Maxwell's hands fly up to his face. He releases a blood-curdling scream. "Why? Why—" he screams again, but this time, it devolves into a laugh. "Why would you think that would actually work? Salt? You trying to season me to death? I mean, death *again*." He laughs even harder at his own awful joke.

I scowl and am about to snap back when a high-pitched beep blares through the kitchen: the smoke alarm.

At my feet, Pao yelps and dashes away. I hear her escape upstairs, and, to my horror, heavy footsteps thunder down.

I stare straight through Maxwell to find Mom at the doorway, her hands flat against her ears. "Barnaby!"

she yells over the alarm. "What in the world are you doing?"

She can't see him. And here I am, alone in a kitchen full of smoke.

If only a handful of salt would banish me far, far away from this place too.

6

I've spent so long in this patio lounge chair this morning that the seat plastic is practically molded to my butt. I consider moving inside, but I'd rather serve my sentence out in the fresh air, with the warm sun and ocean sounds. Inside the attic, I only have uneasy rest and the occasional startle any time Maxwell appears. I don't know what he does when he isn't visible and pestering me, but I don't quite care.

According to Mom, the punishment for nearly setting our vacation rental on fire is twenty-four hours without my tablet. When I pointed out that I merely filled the place with smoke, that turned into forty-eight hours. Dad did nothing to help. It's his name on the rental contract with Mr. Morgan, so as much as he says he feels bad for me, he sides with my mom on this one. Predictable.

My phone buzzes, and I check for any adults before I pull it out of my hoodie pocket. Somehow, in Mom's rage, she forgot to confiscate my phone. So in between sorting through clutter and year-old mail at Grandpa's, I've spent the last day scrolling through the group chat and playing the sole game on my phone—sudoku—until they respond.

Morris: Beware: that latest update took forever to install! Used up almost all my screen time.
Cru: Got it. Will start it now. We're still playing this afternoon, right?
Me: I wish.

I sigh aloud. Between the distance, grounding, and the fact that the connection speeds here are snail slow, I'm stuck as a spectator.

Navigating to Morris's earlier message, I review my options for banishing Maxwell. The last suggestion left is an exorcism, which I'm pretty sure he included as more of a joke. But I'm desperate, after how Maxwell has already managed to wreck the beginning of my summer. Maybe there's some sort of easy "exorcism for beginners" video I can find online.

I'm scrolling through search results when the door from the kitchen to the patio creaks open. I rush to stow my phone. I expect to see Dad with a plate of fruit, but instead, it's Leo. He has a graphic novel tucked under one arm. He scans the patio for a place to sit, then notices me.

"It's nice out here," he says, plopping into the chair next to me. I thought my scowl would be enough to signal that I want to be left alone, but apparently not.

He puts his feet up. "I, um, heard about the fire. I've never seen you cook before. What were you trying to make?"

He and probably the whole block heard my mom detail, very loudly, everything I did wrong and the consequences for it. "Nothing."

"So then why the pans? And the spices?"

I slump down into the chair. I consider telling Leo about the ghost. He has a pretty vivid imagination. He'd believe me. But then he'd probably want to help me get rid of Maxwell or, worse, meet him. More time with my little brother is not how I'd planned on spending the summer.

"If you must know, I was trying to clear the air of, um, negative energy."

Leo raises his eyebrow. "Like smudging? Burning sage?"

My eyes widen. "How—how do you know about that?"

"First of all, read a book, Barnaby," he says with an eye roll. "Second, if you're going to appropriate Indigenous culture, at least get the type of herb right. The house smells like a burnt frozen pizza, and not in a good way."

I have no clue when my little brother got so much smarter than me, but I don't like it. I swing my legs off the side of my chair and pull out my phone to review the exorcism how-to results again. "Right. Well, as much as I love this chat, I'm going inside."

The title of a three-minute video catches my eye: *Cast Out a Ghoul in Four Easy Steps!* Four steps and three minutes? Exactly what I was looking for.

As I head for the patio door, I peer back at Leo and am surprised to catch the slightest hint of sadness on his face.

"You know, if you want to get rid of negative energy, I can help," he says. "Mom took your tablet, but she didn't say you couldn't leave the house. There's a library down the block with fast computers. Plus, Dad says it has a huge graphic novel selection."

"I'll pass." I click on the "Cast Out a Ghoul" video. "Maybe another time."

"We're here for three weeks. We're not even going to Grandpa's today to pack because he and Dad are doing boring paperwork. So why not now?"

"I have stuff to do."

"Like what?"

An exorcism in four easy steps. But I know better than to say that out loud. "Just stuff."

That sadness on his face morphs into anger. "You never want to hang out with me."

"That's not true," I spout out immediately, even though there is some truth to that.

It's not fun having my little brother tag along when I

go out with my friends. I'm already the youngest in our group—I squeaked into seventh grade right at the school's birthday cutoff—and I don't need to remind everyone of that fact. It took me ages to live down walking into the first day of middle school with the babyish *Paw Patrol* backpack Grandma gifted me. There's just too big of a gulf between my twelve years and Leo's nine sometimes.

"I'm busy today."

"We're on vacation, Barnaby. And you're grounded."

I sigh, but it comes out a groan. "Come on, what would we even do? You and I like different things. Books are more your style. Video games are mine—well, if Mom ever gives my tablet back—and you're too young to play the ones I do anyway."

"So? I bet we could find something to do."

I drag a hand through my hair. "Maybe tomorrow, okay?"

Leo's shoulders slump, and he moves to open the book he brought outside. I guess our conversation is over. Good. I have a ghost to cast out.

7

A two-hour arts and crafts session later, I have a homemade Ouija board. The video said I needed to contact the ghost and demand, firmly, that it should leave. There isn't a Ouija board in the house, nor does my grounding allow me to ask for money to go buy one. But one made from cardboard, printer paper, and a nearly dried-up marker will probably work just as well.

The video mentioned opening windows to let in fresh air and as an exit for the offending spirit. The windows in the attic are wide open, and I'm lucky to have strong ocean breezes today. Already the room feels cleaner and less negative. It could be because Maxwell hasn't shown his face yet, though.

The video also said I should light candles, but *I* would join the spirit world if Mom caught me starting more fires in the rental house.

The moment I settle on the floor of the room, Maxwell materializes on the windowsill.

"I'm more of a Monopoly fan myself," he says with a smirk.

A breeze comes through and the curtains flutter, but Maxwell's hair and clothes remain unmoved.

"Of course you'd love a game all about claiming property."

I mean it to be a jab, but Maxwell genuinely laughs. "What's that you have there? A Ouija board? Who are you trying to talk to?"

I position the planchette on the board. "You. Get ready to be exorcised."

"Exercised? Like that Jazzercise my mom used to do?"

"Jazzerwhat? No, I mean *exorcise* as in kick you out of here."

Maxwell hops off the windowsill and approaches me. "Well, that sounds like less fun. Why do you need a board to talk to me, though? We're literally speaking right now."

"It's a process. You wouldn't understand." I barely understand it after a three-minute video, but I'll try anything. "Consider this your last warning. You have two minutes to get out of here or this thing will push you out."

"If this is anything like your seasoning séance earlier, I've gotta see it." He sits directly across the board from me.

My jaw clenches, and I try to focus. The closer he is to the board, the more powerful the effect. I think.

I clear my throat, put my hands on the planchette, and use the script from the video. "Spirit, do you hear me?"

Maxwell grins. "I'm right here. This is silly."

The video said to try to be nice first, so here goes. "Spirit: please leave."

This time, Maxwell snorts. "Um, no. We went through this. I'm staying. You leave."

I scowl. "Then you give me no other choice. You are not welcome here. I demand you leave!"

Maxwell makes no move to exit—willingly or otherwise—but his face settles into a scowl to match mine. "You are really getting annoying."

That was step four: Why isn't he gone? I clear my throat again. "I said, I demand you leave!"

The room goes quiet, except for the sounds of the waves and wind outside. Downstairs, Mom is still locked in the office, clacking away at her laptop with Pao snuggled up by her legs, and Leo fell asleep with a graphic novel on his face. It's just me and Maxwell now, and he's not budging.

Just then, a burst of wind blows through the room. It kicks the curtains up and, to my horror, moves my flimsy homemade Ouija board underneath the planchette I'm holding. I don't see what letters or numbers were touched, but the way Maxwell's jaw drops makes my stomach turn.

I shove the planchette over to my messily scrawled *Goodbye* to turn the whole thing off.

Our eyes meet over the board.

"What—what just happened?" Maxwell asks. He sounds as confused as I feel.

"I don't know. Did you do that wind thing?"

He rolls his eyes. "I could barely open that shrimp chip bag. You seriously think I can control the weather?"

Disappointment washes over me. "Great. I spent all afternoon drawing and cutting, and you're still here. What a waste."

I move to crumple up the board when, suddenly, the fingers on my right hand fling straight out and freeze like I'm waiting for a high five. The breath catches in my throat.

Then Maxwell giggles—*giggles*. He's staring down at my hand, his own in a high-five gesture. He wiggles his fingers up and down, and I'm stunned to see my own fingers move to match his gestures exactly.

"What's happening?" I shriek.

"Oh, this is interesting. Never been able to do this before," Maxwell says, mostly to himself. Then he glances up at me, mischief in his eyes. "A waste? No, I wouldn't call this afternoon a waste. Not at all. I feel better than ever, thanks to you."

I did this? I mutter a silent curse against the "Cast Out a Ghoul" video and my makeshift Ouija board. I grab my right wrist with my left hand in an attempt to get it under control but still can't get my fingers to cooperate. The more I try—and fail—the more I panic.

A ghost I'm at odds with suddenly has control of *my* body? There are so many ways this could go wrong. He's already caused trouble with his own powers, with that shrimp chip disaster. Now what if he tries to hurt me? Or someone else? I need to stop these new ghost powers in their tracks before Maxwell can channel them into getting my family kicked out of Warner Place or me grounded until the end of time.

Working against him clearly didn't succeed, which leaves only one, awful option. It's the approach I'd immediately vetoed because it meant more time with Maxwell: playing nice. If he needs me, he can't hurt or get rid of me, right?

"Stop! I'll—I'll help you!" I practically vomit out. The words taste that bad.

Maxwell—and my own hands—go still. "What did you say?" he asks.

"I'll help you. We can solve your unfinished business and move you on to the afterlife." And out of my hair.

"What makes you think I want to move on? I like it here," he says. It's obvious he's trying to sound confident, but I catch a shakiness in his voice. "It's you who needs to move on out."

"My family's not going anywhere for the next three

weeks. Even if we did leave, Mr. Morgan would probably have another tourist in here by the end of the day."

He stays silent. He's listening.

"What if these new renters aren't some quiet adults and a couple of kids?" I continue. "It could be someone who snores so loud it rattles the windows. Or some nonstop-partying college students. It could get so, so much more unlivable—or, um, unbearable—for you. You don't want to be stuck in this renter lottery for eternity, do you?"

Maxwell crosses his arms. "It *has* been pretty boring in here lately. I've tried to leave, but I can't go past the fence!" His eyes drift to the window. "The beach is right there. And there used to be a comic book store down the block. I'm stuck in this house with this ugly furniture and a TV I don't know how to work."

His words rise in volume as he speaks, and I splay out my hands to placate him. To my relief, my fingers move on my own command. He must have to really concentrate to exert control over me. Riling him up must have distracted him enough for me to take back control.

"Let's get you unstuck, then," I say. "I don't know a lot about where you'll go after this, but it's got to be more interesting than what's within the bounds of this place."

"It has been decades. . . ." Maxwell says, trailing off. He rises and begins to pace, his feet silently padding across the floor. He wanders over to the window, and the billowing curtains float right through him. After a quiet minute, he turns to me. "What would you get out of this?"

"If you want my help, then you have to stop trying to kick me and my family out of here," I say. "And stop this ghost control stuff. Stay out of my body."

His face scrunches like I've stomped on his birthday cake. "Way to ruin all my fun." He sighs, then cocks his head to the side. "Fine. I let you stay and don't try the ghost control, and in exchange, you help me with my unfinished business."

I jut out my hand. "Deal?"

He puts his own ghost hand through mine, and it's icy where our palms would've met in a handshake. "Deal."

8

My hand trembles as I lift the glass of lemonade. Sugar is a must after the deal I was forced to make.

Across the coffee table from me looms Maxwell. From my spot on the living room couch, I can see the stairs, the gigantic television, and tall potted plant behind his translucent form. He must mean for me to start this unfinished-business business right away. If I'm going to have to work closely with him, I need to set some boundaries.

I lower my glass. "Let's lay out some rules. No bothering or trying out your powers on anyone else in my family. This includes Pao, our dog. Nothing can *ever* happen to the dog, got it?"

He starts to answer, but I continue. The thought of Maxwell messing with my hair on the video call with my friends comes to mind. Spending hours of my life in the back seat while Mom took her work calls over speakerphone made some basic negotiation skills sink in. "And no pestering me in front of them so I get in trouble, okay?"

Maxwell nods. "My turn. The deal is you helping me: if you try to exorcise me again, the deal is off."

"All right. And no taking over my body with your"—I flutter my fingers in the air because I really don't have a good phrase for this—"ghost control. I don't know what I did with that Ouija board to trigger this power, but I don't like it."

He looks annoyed that I've brought it up again. "Fine, but remember: no help, no deal."

We eye each other; it's a little odd with me sitting and him standing. I guess it would be weird if he sat in one of the chairs near me, though. I don't know if he even needs to sit or worry about energy or aches like that.

Satisfied that I have his cooperation, I pull out my phone. "Then let's get started. What's the business that you need to finish?"

"I think it has something to do with why I'm stuck in this house specifically, like there's something here I'm missing."

"You don't know for sure?"

"If I did, don't you think I would've done it already so I could stop hanging out here all by myself?"

He makes a good point, one that I should have thought about before I blurted out this vow to help him. It's still not a bad deal, if it means I retain control of my body and keep my family safe. I can't help the rising annoyance at his attitude, though.

"If only I could figure out what I was doing before I died. When I finally found myself back in my room in ghost form, it was five years later. My parents were gone. There was an entirely new family here." Maxwell sighs. "If I could find my parents and speak with them, they could fill in the blanks of the time I missed. We could piece together what my unfinished business is."

"But you can touch things—you ripped open the chip bag. Couldn't you just use that new family's phone to call your parents?"

Maxwell shakes his head. "I died December 1984. Regular people didn't carry around phones in their pockets like you all do now. Once my family moved, they got a new phone number."

"And it's not like they thought to write it down and leave it here for you," I say quietly to myself. Despite how annoying I find Maxwell, I feel sad for him. He is—was—a kid just like me, with a life, a family, neighbors, friends. But tragedy struck and he lost everything. I clear my throat, hoping some of the unbidden sympathy goes with it. "So what happened to you in 1984? Do you think that has something to do with your unfinished business?"

"I got sick. A stomach bug. Then I died. What's unfinished about that?"

He doesn't want to go into detail, and I don't want to push it. I can't get sidetracked this early. This ghost was dead set on making me miserable an hour ago. I'm not here to win friends: I'm here to get my room—and my summer—back.

"But I must be missing something, something big. The hours before I died are a blur. I remember the usual stuff like going to school, riding home with my dad . . . but the rest of it is hazy. I'm sure my parents would remember."

"Okay, then let's start by looking them up. You said you can't leave the property, so maybe we can ask your family to come back here instead."

Maxwell perks up. "Yeah, let's do that. Their names are Gene and Joyce Warner. He was in construction, like my grandfather. She was a secretary at the high school and town baking champion four years in a row for her 'Joyous' key lime pie."

The key lime pie—that must have been the mysterious scent from the pantry, even though it's been decades since Joyce Warner baked a pie in this house.

Maxwell continues. "They were at least here until 1984, but I don't know when they would've moved. Hey, aren't you going to write any of this down?"

I type away on my phone. "I am. I'm putting their names into a search."

He mouths a *wow*. I forget that he grew up without the entire world's information at his fingertips. I must seem so powerful to him right now. Good. The more useful I am, the less he's going to want to mess with me.

The results load, and I frown at the dozens of names on the page, none of them a perfect match for Maxwell's parents.

"What's wrong?" he asks. He disappears for a moment. When he suddenly reappears over my shoulder, staring at my phone, I force myself not to jump. "Don't—don't do that! Or at least give me a warning before you zip around."

Maxwell huffs. "You looked upset at your phone. What happened?"

I angle the screen so he can read it. "I didn't get any direct hits, which is weird. I'm good at this. I was able to track down my PE teacher's ex-girlfriend in three minutes when he needed an old yearbook back. But your parents' names aren't showing up anywhere. Did I spell everything right?"

Maxwell hovers over my phone and lets out a growl. "Yes, that's right." Then he glares at me. "You said you'd help!"

"I *am* helping!" I draw my phone back. "But I don't control search results. They must not be online much. That makes them a lot harder to find."

Maxwell crosses his arms. The television flickers on,

and I stare at the remote control on the coffee table. I hadn't touched it.

"Was that you?" I ask.

"Everyone is all high-tech this, high-tech that these days," he says instead of answering my question. The television begins to switch from channel to channel, the volume rising.

"Hey, stop it!" I lunge for the remote. "My mom is working right upstairs!"

I press the mute button, but Maxwell somehow overrides it. We battle over control of the television. He settles on a channel that's showing last year's big dragon battle movie. I'd wanted to see it in theaters, but my parents had said no because of the intense amount of gore and cursing—all of which is in showcased in wall-shaking surround sound right this minute.

I don't need Mom emerging from her office again to investigate the screeching of dragons gnashing people to bits or the bellowing of four-letter words I'm not even allowed to think.

I mash at the remote, but it's no use. I hop up and wave my hands in front of his face. "Maxwell, it's okay, calm down. I said it'll be harder, not impossible."

Distracted, he loses his ghost-power hold on the television, and the mute function finally kicks in.

"You have to help me. That was the deal," he spits out.

"I will. But I can't if that noise bothers my mom and I

get in trouble. Also, this is one fancy television but I don't think it's going to track down your parents, so leave the poor thing alone."

Maxwell uncrosses his arms and grumbles to himself, his ghost tantrum waning. He still looks upset, but less ready to explode.

"I-I'm sorry. How am I supposed to know how everything works?" he says. "Even the new refrigerator in the kitchen has a screen and a thousand different buttons on the front. Can you use that in our search?"

I try to stifle my laugh. "I don't think so."

He groans. "Then what good is any of this new stuff? I thought I was missing out on not being able to work the high-tech machines they put into this house, but maybe not."

"Well, the fridge screen can tell you the temperature inside so your eggs don't go bad."

Maxwell's expression goes flat. "You mean all these years I've been dead, *that*'s the best the world could come up with? Please at least tell me that hoverboards exist."

I rub the back of my neck. "Hoverboards do exist, but people don't really use them."

"Why not?" he asks, incredulous. "My friends and I wished so hard those would get invented!"

"Their batteries kept exploding!" a voice chimes in way too happily from the stairs.

Maxwell and I both turn, but I know that voice.

Halfway down the staircase, Leo stands with an armful of graphic novels.

I gulp. How much did my brother hear, and how bizarre did my seemingly one-sided conversation sound?

"I-I'm thinking about getting a hoverboard for myself, and I heard that the best way to figure out pros and cons is to argue it out . . . with yourself . . . out loud." I'm babbling, but I can't stop. I need my little brother to just forget what he witnessed.

"Oh, interesting tactic. That makes sense," Leo says, "Good luck getting Mom and Dad to buy you one, though. If you play your cards right, Grandpa might."

Before I can breathe out a sigh of relief, I realize he hasn't made any move to ascend the stairs yet. "What do you need?" I ask, hoping to hurry him away.

"I need you to not be rude. Aren't you going to introduce me to your friend?" He stares straight at the spot where Maxwell stands. "Hi. My name's Leo."

The delight on Maxwell's face must be the polar opposite of the horror on mine.

The ghost floats forward and waves. "And I'm Maxwell. So glad to meet you."

9

I'm not the best big brother in the world.

I despise taking turns. I eat all the marshmallow bits out of the cereal box when no one is looking. I always snag the window seat when we're on a plane or train.

Even then, I'm pretty sure Leo and a ghost bent on kicking us out shouldn't mix.

"Leo, leave," I say, a little more forcefully than I intended.

Somehow, Leo sees Maxwell too. But if Leo hasn't picked up on any ghostly vibes from Maxwell, I'm not about to point them out. Let him believe there's a random, live kid in the house. That's easier to make up excuses about.

My brother's mouth dips down at the corners. "Why? Why can't I hang out with you and your friend? You never let me."

I ignore the pang of guilt because it's partially true. Who wants a younger brother tagging along and cramping their style? But a glance at Maxwell ignites that protective streak in me. Maxwell is staring at Leo like he's the one piece of good Halloween chocolate in a sea of stale candy corn.

The ghost grins, mischief sparkling in his slightly see-through eyes. "Yes, let him hang out with us, Barnaby."

I whirl to glare at him. "I said no pestering my family."

"He said hi first, and he wants to spend time with us," Maxwell says. "That's not pestering."

I huff, which only causes Maxwell's grin to spread. I angle to see behind Leo, hoping some responsible adult will whisk my little brother away. But Dad is still off with Grandpa, and Mom is locked in the office, hard at work. I also can't kick my little brother out of the house into the middle of an unfamiliar town.

"Why don't you go read outside on the beach? Far away from the house. But, um, not so far that I can't see you."

My brother doesn't seem to sense what I'm trying to do. "Your friend—"

In a matter of seconds, I've leaped across the living room and tugged Leo down the rest of the stairs, out the front door, and to the sidewalk at the edge of the driveway. Hopefully we're outside the property line and Maxwell can't reach us here.

"My book!" Leo says, his arm stretching toward the graphic novel that had tumbled off his stack and is lying in our driveway. "I'm telling Mom you're being mean and not letting me hang out—"

"Leo, no, you're not getting it. That kid up there is bad news. I don't want you anywhere near him."

"Why do you get to be friends with him and I can't?"

"We're not friends." I force myself to release my clenched jaw.

But my brother ignores my words and defaults back to his eternally cheery side. "If we get to know some more kids around here, maybe they'll be up for helping Grandpa pack too! Let's go inside and talk to—"

"No. We don't need him or anyone else around here. We're only in Sunnyside until Grandpa's moved out, then we get to go home. Why don't you go bury yourself in all those books until it's time to leave, okay?"

"You're kind of a jerk, you know that? You're so grumpy these days, and you take it out on everyone else," Leo snaps at me.

The way his face pinches makes me realize I've probably said exactly the wrong things. If I was trying to convince Leo that I wasn't trying to exclude him, then I'm failing horribly.

I hadn't wanted Maxwell messing with my little brother, but I went and crushed Leo's feelings all by myself. Maybe I should switch tacks and let Leo help. I could keep an eye on both him and Maxwell and make sure that ghost doesn't pull anything sneaky behind my back. Also, selfishly, by bringing Leo in—and on my own terms—my brother won't gripe to Mom that I'm excluding him. As a general rule, everyone is all around happier and life is easier when Mom isn't angry.

I rub the back of my neck. "Look, I—I'm sorry. I just don't want anything to happen to you."

The ocean wind picks up and, despite the summer warmth, it sends goose bumps rippling down my arms.

Leo shivers too. "Wait, why would anything happen to me? Is this about that kid in our house?"

"He's not just some kid. . . ." I draw in a breath to steel myself. "He's a ghost, and the house—he thinks it's his."

"No. Way." Leo's eyes widen with each word, his reaction the opposite of Dad's. He believes me. "The negative energy you almost set the kitchen on fire for! Was it because of him?"

I nod. "I was trying to banish him, but it backfired. I really messed up. So I agreed to help him so that he'd stop trying to get us kicked out of the house."

"You're going to solve his unfinished business?"

My jaw goes slack. "Wait, you know about unfinished business?"

Technically, I shouldn't be this surprised that a kid

who always has his nose in a book or pressed against a YouTube screen would know as much about ghosts as movie-fiend Morris.

Leo rolls his eyes. "Oh. Wow. You really need my help if you don't even understand basics like that."

The corner of my mouth ticks up. I'm thankful that my little brother spared me from having to ask him for help. He simply volunteered it. Is he so starved for hangout time that he's willing to go up against a ghost with me?

"It wouldn't hurt to have you on my team, especially since you seem to know so much about the otherworldly. Plus if we need any more info, you can add whatever you want to your e-library cart. Dad never checks your stuff."

Leo smiles. "I'm not the one who borrowed a whole true-crime series and slept with a baseball bat nearby for a month. But, actually, I have to ask—you said something could happen to us. Is this ghost dangerous?"

A shiver runs down my back. I stare at the house, my eyes going to the top windows where my room would be. I don't see anyone, but part of me knows Maxwell is there, possibly watching my brother and me right this moment.

"I don't know," I say. Maxwell's power has grown, thanks to my Ouija board mistake, but now we have a mutual goal and a deal sealed with a handshake. Though it makes me uneasy that I don't know enough about Maxwell to know how reliable his word is. He already found a loophole with my "pestering" rule.

My brother purses his lips.

I put my hand on his shoulder. "But let's not wait to find out, okay? Let's get to the bottom of this unfinished business so we can send him off to heaven or—"

"To *h–e*–double hockey sticks," Leo finishes with a fist pump, carefully balancing his stack of graphic novels on his other arm. "I'm in."

We turn back to the house, and I pick up the dropped graphic novel on the way. Something flickers in the top window, and I swallow down the worry that we don't know who—or what—we're dealing with.

10

As we stow Leo's books in his room, the door to the office creaks open. For a moment, I wonder if Maxwell has somehow broken our deal and gotten to my mom, and I'm about to dash over there to chase him off. Then Mom emerges, her hands on her lower back, stretching. Her hair is pulled into a thick bun that's messy in a way that probably isn't on purpose. Pao trots out of the office behind her.

"Hey, you two, I need a favor," Mom asks, her voice weary. She's been on phone calls for the past few hours, which thankfully has kept her unaware of my dealings with Maxwell.

Pao plants her furry butt on the floor and yawns, equally exhausted from listening to Mom yammer all day.

"Sure!" Leo blurts out the same time I grumble, "I'm busy."

Mom somehow manages to smile at Leo while rolling her eyes at me. That level of body language is a superpower.

"Go down to the market on the corner and pick up a few things for dinner. The market is circled on the map Mr. Morgan put on the fridge for us. I was hoping to go right now, but my boss just surprised me by scheduling another meeting, and I can't step away."

Actually, a Mom-sanctioned excursion out of Maxwell's reach isn't a terrible suggestion. "Fine. What do you need?"

Mom steps back into the office and returns with her purse. She hands me some cash. "Parmesan, a jar of marinara sauce, and a box of spaghetti."

I count the bills. "Is it really going to cost this much? Wouldn't it make more sense to buy already-cooked spaghetti from a restaurant?"

"Why, when I can just make it at home?"

"Why, when you can just buy it from a restaurant?"

"Enough, Barnaby. I'm cooking tonight," Mom says, impatient. "Actually, buy some oregano too. I think you burned all of it with that little science experiment of yours."

Next to me, Leo stifles a giggle. "Do you want to come, Pao?"

He squats down to pet Pao, who is already wagging her tail. Normally, I'd be annoyed that my brother is trying to make this a group activity when all I want to do is be alone, but I secretly adore that little furry face—Pao's, not my brother's—and honestly, everyone in our house needs to get away from Maxwell.

Mom shakes her head. "Sorry, I don't think they'll let dogs into the store, near all the food."

I stuff the cash into my pocket. "Anything else while we're out?"

"Maybe something for dessert. Something healthy."

"Those are two opposite things."

This time, Mom just sighs. "I have to join this call. I want to get cooking at five, so try to be back before then. Text me if you need anything."

I head to the kitchen to locate Mr. Morgan's map. Leo scurries over to the closet to grab a windbreaker. Of course he thought to pack a jacket, even though it's a solid eighty degrees outside.

"There it is, Fern's Grocery. It's not too far," I say, scanning the cartoony map created by the Sunnyside Tourism Bureau.

Grainy clip art of seagulls hovers over the bright blue ocean, and Mr. Morgan has drawn a big red star over where our house is. The market is only three blocks away. I must've passed it on my walks with Pao. I don't recognize some of the other names on the map, like Icky's Ice Cream Parlor and the Ye Olde Hot Dog Kingdom. They must have all gone out of business.

"Come on, we can take the scenic route along the boardwalk," I say. I reach for our neon-orange reusable bag, but Leo already has it.

Together, we exit out the back door and let it smack shut behind us.

"Ouch, son of a—" someone yips next door.

Before I can stop him, Leo calls out, "Do you need help?"

We haven't even left the backyard, and our shopping trip is already derailed. I peek up at the second floor, at the window of the room Mom uses as an office. She's pacing and waving her hands around as she talks—one of those waves is for me when she notices I'm looking. My gaze drifts up to the attic window above, and for a moment I think I see a shadow. Is Maxwell watching?

I'd rather not spend an extra minute even thinking about that ghost, so I gently nudge Leo out of the back gate and safely off Warner Place property. On the plus side, at least Maxwell can't get to us here. But a decidedly not-plus is that now we're in full view of the yipping neighbor.

She's a Black woman in her seventies, with curly white hair cropped close, topped by a floppy straw sun hat. She cradles one of her hands with the other gardening-gloved one. When our gate clicks shut, she turns at the noise and smiles at my brother and me.

"Why, yes, I actually could use your help, if you've got a minute," she says.

I don't even bother stopping my brother from blurting out, "Of course! I'm Leo. We're renting this house for a few weeks."

Then he elbows me.

"Oh. Hi. I'm Barnaby."

The woman smiles warmly. "Pleasure to meet you both. I'm Anita. It's nice to see some young folks next door. It's been ages since we've had children in this neighborhood. It's mostly retirees and spring breakers these days." She pulls off her other glove and tucks both under her arm. "Would you be able to switch off that faucet and coil up my garden hose? Overdid the yard work today, and my arthritis is acting up."

Sounds easy—and quick—enough. I stride down the uneven stone walkway through her small backyard and put some muscle into turning the faucet handle closed. Leo and Ms. Anita keep chatting by the gate.

"Our grandpa has arthritis too. He has some big handle thing on his outdoor faucet at his house over on Cedar Street. That handle might be helpful for yours," Leo says.

Ms. Anita raises an eyebrow. "On Cedar, hmm? What's his name?"

"Albert Vargas," I volunteer.

Her brown eyes light up. "Al! He and your grandmother were regulars at the café my daughter used to work at. So sorry to hear about your grandmother. She was such a kind lady."

I never know how to respond when people offer me condolences, so I dodge the topic altogether. I finish coiling the hose. "We're here helping Grandpa pack up his house."

"Ah. Everyone's moving out of Sunnyside," she says, her voice quieting. Then she seems to shake off the momentary gloom. "Thanks so much for your help, Barnaby and Leo. Feel free to stop by anytime, if your parents don't mind you helping me in the garden. I can pay you in chocolate."

Leo's eyes widen at the mention of chocolate, and I know we'll be back. I join him at the gate while Ms. Anita showers us with a few more thank-yous and tips about Sunnyside life, like how we must try Mr. Yen's fresh noodles at the weekend farmers market.

I'm about to take off down the boardwalk when something she said earlier tickles the back of my mind. "Um, Ms. Anita?" I call to her.

She has already turned to go back into her house, but she pauses and glances over her shoulder at me. "Yes?"

"You said it's been a while since there were kids around here. I—I found a stack of old baseball cards up in the attic and figured whatever kid used to live here might want them," I lie. I just met the lady—I'm not about to surprise her with a story about her ghost neighbor. "Would you happen to know where the family is? So I can return the cards, I mean."

Her earlier gloom returns, a heavy wrinkle settling between her brows. "The Warners. What a lovely family. Their poor, poor boy." Then she goes silent, lost in whatever thoughts she can't bear to voice.

Goose bumps spread down my neck. It's not that Ms. Anita told us anything too scary or suspicious about Maxwell, but her not telling us much might also mean something. I exchange a look with Leo. He's better than me at getting new people to open up.

Leo coughs to clear his throat. "Do you know where we can find that boy?" He and I both know exactly where Maxwell is—haunting my attic room and possibly spying on us right now—but thankfully Leo knows as well as I do to be careful with who we mention ghosts to. "Or his parents?"

"Hmm. You know, it's been such a long time since—"

"Leo, Barnaby, get moving!" Mom suddenly calls from her office window. Then she notices Ms. Anita and quickly adds, "Oh, sorry! I didn't realize they were with you."

Whatever Ms. Anita was going to share with us promptly gets locked back in her brain. Her cheery disposition returns, and she waves at Mom. "Not a problem, dear. I'll let these boys go on their way."

With Mom watching us, we say goodbye to our neighbor and trudge down the boardwalk to the market.

As we walk, my skin prickles with the sense that another pair of eyes follows us from the house, and I'm pretty sure they're not Pao's.

11

We're wonderfully Maxwell-free until the next afternoon. Leo and I sprawl over the lounge chairs in the backyard, waiting for the hot tub to heat up. I wanted to go to the beach, outside of the fence and far from Maxwell's reach, but lifeguard trainees are swarming the coast, running drills. I wasn't about to get mowed over by a gaggle of teenagers in red Speedos.

But because basking in the sunshine is too good to be true, Maxwell materializes in front of us. He obscures our view of the Speedoed lifeguards, which isn't necessarily a bad thing. His arms are crossed, and I can already tell by his scowl what kind of mood he's in.

Leo doesn't have as good of a grumpiness radar as I do. "Maxwell! How can we help you?"

A snort escapes me. "Help? 'Help' makes it sound like

he's not holding us hostage and forcing us to figure out his unfinished business."

"A ghost's gotta do what a ghost's gotta do," Maxwell says with a shrug. "You think I *want* to hang out in your smelly body?"

I sit up. "I'm not smelly!"

"You didn't shower today. Or yesterday."

My jaw drops. "Are you—are you spying on me? That's super creepy!"

"Don't flatter yourself. You're as boring as you are smelly."

Next to me, Leo stifles a giggle, then forces his face into a serious expression, as if he didn't take sides with a ghost over his own brother.

I glare at Maxwell. "How can you even smell? You don't have a body."

"And thank heavens for that. I can't imagine how bad the stench would be if I did. That doesn't mean I can't see the comic book–style stink lines radiating off you."

Before I volley back an insult, Leo splays out his arms. "All right, enough. Seriously, how am I the youngest one here but somehow the most mature?"

"Well, I'm only three years old than you," I say.

"And I'm only two . . . Oh," Maxwell says, trailing off.

The realization takes all the fight out of me. He's not only two years older than my brother. He's two years and over four decades older, forever frozen as the ghost of an eleven-year-old.

"Comic book stink lines," Leo says with a snicker. His laugh dials down the tension in the backyard. "Hey, Maxwell, if you're a comic book fan, you might like these." My brother nudges the graphic novel next to him.

I raise my eyebrow. "Can you even pick up the book and flip the pages, Maxwell?"

"Sure I can. It takes some energy, but I ripped open that shrimp chip bag, didn't I?"

"Don't remind me," I groan.

Maxwell approaches Leo's graphic novel. "I saw you had a stack of those. Are they any good?"

"Only the best series ever!" my brother responds, his eyes wide. "You can borrow them anytime."

"That'd be awesome!" Maxwell says.

Then his smile dims a few watts. My brother doesn't notice, but I do, and I wonder why. I doubt Maxwell has had access to any new, interesting books like this in a while. The only books in the living room bookcase are old romance novels and thrillers that aren't exactly targeted toward eleven-year-olds. I also get the sense that Leo, with his quick smile and never-ending generosity, may be the first kid in ages to offer to share anything with him.

"What is it that you do when you're not monitoring my shower habits?" I ask. Maxwell isn't always around—thank goodness—but I've wondered where exactly he is when I can't see him.

He rolls his eyes. "I can fade into my version of the house, the house in 1984. Back when it was renter-free and I had my *E.T.* poster on the wall. No one's there, though, just me. So no, I'm not always lurking around monitoring your shower habits."

"Good. But why don't you stay there? I don't mean that in a rude way, but if it's peaceful, why not hang out there instead of here?"

"Well, I can get yanked back into this reality by loud, annoying noises like a door slamming or karaoke or someone's snoring."

He sends a pointed glare at me, and Leo laughs again. These two teaming up against me? Unfair.

Then Maxwell clears his throat. "So have you found any leads on my family?"

Because I don't have the heart to tell him no, I pop up from my lounge chair. "Down to business already, hmm? How about we take this conversation to the hot tub?"

At the suggestion, Leo scampers over to the tub.

The hot tub sits close to the fence on the other side of the backyard, away from Ms. Anita's house. An oversize red patio umbrella shades half the water, and next to it stands a short metal rack that doubles as cleaning supply storage and hot-tub drink and snack holder.

Steam rises from the bubbling surface of the water, and the scent of chlorine mixes with the briny ocean air. I place my glass of lemonade on the metal rack and ball my towel up next to it. Leo dips into the tub first and practically melts into a relaxed blob as he settles in.

I seat myself opposite him, close my eyes, and release a long breath. My moment of relaxation ends all too quickly when I open my eyes and see Maxwell perched on the edge of the tub, his ghost feet in the water right next to me.

I know he's not really in the water, but I don't love the idea of the kid's feet so close to my face. I purposefully float a few inches away.

"So. My family. Anything?" Maxwell asks.

"I set up some search engine alerts on your family, but nothing new since the other day."

"Search engine alert? What does that mean?"

"It means it'll tell us if any new mentions of your family show up online," Leo pipes up. "But seeing as how there isn't anything out there on them already, the chances seem pretty low."

Maxwell's face scrunches. "That's all? Your plan is to sit around and wait until this alarm goes off?"

"It's not exactly an alarm. It's an email," Leo explains. "So more like a gentle ping." My brother even says *ping* in a melodious, high-pitched way.

"A *ping*?"

Getting Maxwell even more despondent seems like a terrible idea, so I cut in. "We did talk to Ms. Anita, your neighbor."

At this, Maxwell pauses, and it's like watching a tank grind to a stop. "And?"

"She remembers you! And your family."

He gulps. "Does—does she know where they went?" His voice is quieter, like he's afraid of the answer.

I wish I had thought this line through. If a mere search engine alert upset him, he's going to grumble at this lack of progress too. "I . . . I don't know. Maybe? She sounds like she might know something, but we had to go buy pasta stuff."

His eyes widen. "Pasta. Stuff." He enunciates each syllable. "I have been trapped as a ghost in this house for over forty years, and there might finally be someone who can help, and you . . . You. Go. Buy. Pasta. Stuff."

The dismay in each word makes me want to sink deeper into the hot tub. Across from me, Leo's brow knits with worry. He's not the one at risk of a ghost taking over his body, though, thanks to my deal with Maxwell.

My right arm starts to tingle in a familiar and horrifying way. Not just my fingers either, like when Maxwell took over the first time. This time it's my entire arm, all the way to my shoulder.

"What— Quit it!" I yell, unable to keep the panic from leaking into my words. I try to move my arm, to make sure it's still under my control, but it doesn't respond the way I'd hoped.

Maxwell's brow is pinched in way that looks desperate—and desperate is not a good thing for a body-controlling ghost to be. "I'm sorry, Barnaby, but you said you'd help! You two aren't taking this seriously enough!"

"We are!" I say. "It takes time. We'll do our best while we're here—"

Maxwell's gaze centers on me. "But that's the problem. You're only in town for a few more weeks. I need you at the house, where I can see you and make sure you're working on my unfinished business. I need you"—his eyes flit to the storage rack, and my stomach drops—"grounded."

My arm shoots out to the second level of the rack. I try to stop my right arm by grabbing it with my left hand, but Maxwell is more powerful than he was the other day. My right hand closes over a bottle handle and jerks it up into the air. In the sun, the plastic shines, and a green liquid sloshes around inside.

Dish soap.

Leo splashes over to me and grabs my right arm. "Barnaby, what are you doing? What's happening?"

I hadn't told him about Maxwell's abilities. And I don't get a chance to explain because Maxwell whips my hand to the right and smashes the bottle against the side of the hot tub. The cap goes flying off, and green dish soap gurgles into the hot tub.

Leo's sudden look of horror can't be anywhere near as striking as mine. The bubbles that had once been so soothingly light and effervescent suddenly start multiplying. None of them pop. Leo lurches away, backing up against the edge of the tub as if the soap bubbles are acid.

"Why did you do that?" he shrieks.

"It wasn't me!"

Leo scrambles out of the tub before the bubbles reach him. "But the soap—I saw you do it!"

The back door flies open, and Mom rushes out. Her face is tinged red, like she'd sensed Leo's fear and darted downstairs as fast as humanly possible. "Saw who do what?"

I don't even get a moment to explain. When Mom sees the monstrous amount of bubbles spilling over the sides of the tub, she screams, "Barnaby! What on earth have you done?"

The fact that she assumes this was my fault stings more than it should. Okay, I *have* been grumpy and maybe a little too obviously unhappy to be here, but why would I ruin a perfectly good hot tub?

I force myself out of the water, and the bubbles cling to me like I'm cosplaying a marshmallow. Mom's wild eyes pin me, expecting the best ever explanation for what she's seeing. My shock over Maxwell's antics mixes with the sheer dread of knowing how utterly unbelievable this situation is.

I could flat-out say, "Mom, I'm being terrorized by a vacation-rental ghost who is slowly taking over my body! He's to blame for all the expensive damage to this hot tub and yard."

However, I know Mom. As unfair as it is, the moment this scene sank into her brain, she decided what happened. Mom must think this is all part of some master plan to leave Sunnyside and head home, or, worse, exact revenge on my parents for making us come here.

The punishment for this hot-tub bubble overflow is already going to be awful; I can't imagine how much worse it will be if I bring a ghost story into the mix.

I grit my teeth. I really have no choice other than to keep Maxwell a secret from my parents. I can't solve his unfinished business if they lock me up in the attic.

I blow out a breath, the lie like a mouthful of sand under those Speedoed lifeguards' feet. "I didn't mean to. It was an accident."

I barely hear Mom's *How could you do this?* rant because I focus instead on Maxwell, who leans against the storage rack. A thin layer of bubbles creeps toward his feet and goes straight through them. He kicks at them, but of course they don't move.

"Sorry, but I need you here to focus on my unfinished business. I hope you understand. And, hey, at least you won't have to take a shower today after all," he says with a sheepish smile.

This ghost has got to go.

12

When Dad opens the front door the next morning, I expect to see the plumber. But there's someone else too.

This man seems stylish and out of place in casual Sunnyside, with his glossy, wavy hair, his navy-blue suit, and a crisp white shirt with the top button left undone. A white silk handkerchief with tiny blue anchors on it is folded neatly in his jacket pocket. He and the plumber might be wearing the first closed-toed shoes I've seen since we arrived in this beach town. The plumber, I understand—safety first and everything—but I wouldn't want to imprison my toes if I didn't need to.

Dad thrusts out his hand. "Mr. Morgan, hello! You didn't have to come out here personally. We're so sorry for the trouble."

So *that's* the landlord Maxwell hates. Odd that Dad

was so formal in calling him *Mr.* when they look equally ancient, somewhere in the realm of the early forties.

The man in the suit flashes a gleaming smile at Dad as he shakes his hand. "Please, call me Troy. We're not so formal here in Sunnyside." And yet, he is wearing a suit that is probably more expensive than everything I brought with me. As if he senses me judging him, his green eyes flit in my direction. "And this must be Barnaby."

I wince as he says my name. He scrutinizes me like he's trying to see into my soul to figure out why I'd ruin his vacation property. I begin to apologize for the over-bubbled hot tub. He stops me short when he pats me briefly on the shoulder.

"Don't worry, you're not in trouble. I used to cause my dad much bigger headaches when I was your age," he says with a laugh. "Let me guess: You wanted to impress some friends?"

"I don't have any friends here." And I'm not looking to make any. In fact, I'm trying—and failing—to spend more time alone.

Mr. Morgan snickers. "Ah, a lone wolf. Just like me. Anyway, this isn't the first time Gus"—he juts a thumb out at the plumber behind him—"has had to fix up the tub. We had a bachelor party just last month that clogged up the filter with an unsettling amount of soggy nachos."

The tension melts out of my shoulders at Mr. Morgan's

casual demeanor. When Mom had mentioned the landlord might come to inspect the damage himself, I assumed I was about to be yelled at by someone gruff and Scrooge-like. I hadn't expected the expensive fix to be so quickly glossed over by an easy-laughing, suit-wearing businessman who looks like he stepped straight out of a reality show.

I don't understand Maxwell's hatred of the guy. Then again, there's a lot about Maxwell that I simply don't understand.

"Mind if we take a look?" Gus asks.

Dad steps aside and lets the Gus the plumber and Mr. Morgan in.

Mr. Morgan hands Dad a rolled-up newspaper. "Grabbed this for you on the way here. A little piece of Sunnyside."

Dad smiles. "This town has an actual printed newspaper?"

"It's mostly ads and event listings these days, but we do like our *Sunnyside Gazette*. Keeps this town feeling cozy."

As Dad unrolls the newspaper, I angle to let Gus and Mr. Morgan by. Dad plucks the comics section out for Leo and tucks the rest under his arm.

By the stairs, a floor plank squeaks as Mr. Morgan passes over it. He pauses. "I forgot about that part of the floor. It's been years since I've been in here."

"Did you oversee the renovation yourself?" Dad asks.

"In a way," Mr. Morgan responds. "My dad fixed up the place when I was a boy, and he took me along with him. Even let me swing a hammer once or twice. We kept the place pretty close to the original—mostly cleaned it up and made it safer. Renters like that vintage beach charm."

The air around me goes inexplicably cold, and it's then that I notice Maxwell at the top of the stairs. His mouth a tight line, he glares down at Mr. Morgan. Then my right arm begins to tingle.

Oh no, he can't be trying to control me right now. The last thing I need is for Maxwell to smack Mr. Morgan and get me and my family into real trouble. I cross my arms tight, hoping I can somehow fight back this ghost.

Dad sees the movement and my slow inching toward the stairs. "Barnaby, can you let your mom know Mis—Troy is here?"

My right arm twitches, and I'm barely able to hold it against my chest. I can't see Mom like this. The woman magically knows when I'm faking a cough to avoid soccer practice. She'll know straight away that something is off with my arm. I need to get to the attic and barricade myself in there until the coast is clear. Is this how werewolves feel on a full-moon night?

"I—um—bathroom! Now!" I shriek.

I dash up the stairs, my cheeks burning. How was needing to use the bathroom the first excuse that popped into my mind? Too late now. I'm just going to have to live with the fact that everyone thinks I have a toilet-related emergency. It's either that or risk assaulting that nice landlord.

I'm running toward the stairs to the attic when Leo's bedroom door swings open and he yanks me inside. He slams the door behind us, pressing his back against it.

"What—what are you doing?"

Leo slides down to the floor, sitting between me and the door. "I'm guessing the ghost had something to do with the bubbles. And if that's the case, you probably don't need to be down there while they're trying to fix it."

My little brother's deductive skills impress me. "You're right. It was Maxwell. I messed up a Ouija board thing and now he's slowly taking over my body."

Leo's eyes widen. "Oh. Wow. I knew he could move small stuff like books and chip bags, which is terrifying already. But this weird slow-possession thing is a whole other level of creepy."

"All the more reason to hurry up with my unfinished business!" Maxwell demands, and he's suddenly there, sitting on my brother's bed next to a stack of graphic novels.

I stomp over to him. "Getting me grounded is not helpful! We already told you we did everything we could online. We *have* to leave the house to find more."

Maxwell huffs. I should've anticipated this, given how little he understands about the internet or computers in general. I let my anger stamp out that inkling of pity.

"I wanted to speed up the process, and you have to admit it worked: now that awful Mr. Morgan is here. You can go ask him about my family."

His eyes shift away at the mention of his family, and it's not him being sentimental. Maxwell is up to something.

"No way. I'm not going down there. You're going to do something to that guy, I know it."

Maxwell's continued silence means I'm right.

"He seems nice," I say, "but probably not nice enough to forgive a dropkick or a bite or whatever you've got in mind. So nope, I'm staying in here. You should've thought that bubble thing through. All you've done is make it worse for yourself—for us."

I hop onto the bed, with my arms still tightly woven.

Maxwell's eyes narrow, and I can sense the pull on my arm growing stronger.

"He's not nice," he growls. "He ruined my *home*. There was a kind, quiet family here after mine. But then the Morgans bought this house. They tore out everything that was good and cozy and replaced it with this trash." He gestures at the generic seashell art on the wall and the *Life is better at the beach* sign. "Then came the endless spring breakers, the loud middle-aged ladies on girls' trips who think they can sing . . . I haven't had any rest since he took over!"

It's hard to be sympathetic when someone is threatening to take over your body just to make a point. "Then why haven't you told him all this yourself? If you hate Mr. Morgan so much, why haven't you haunted his butt out of here?"

"That's right," Leo pipes in, from his seat still in front of the door. "You seem to be able to choose who can see you. So why haven't you shown yourself to him and talked this out?"

"You don't think I've tried? I spoke to him the first time he strolled in here in a business suit. Our families have history; we've all been in Sunnyside a long time. I thought he was nice, just like you did. He listened to me, he said he'd help. But then he turned around and tried to exorcise me. Never trusting adults again."

At the flare of Max's frustration, my arm begins to pull away from my body on its own. He's stronger. I struggle to wrangle my own arm, and sweat starts to bead at my temples. Thankfully, Maxwell's concentration is interrupted by the slam of a door downstairs. Leo and I lock eyes. Who could this be?

"Boys!" My grandfather's voice booms up the stairs, as loud as the door slam and the stomp of his footsteps. He never does anything quietly, and for once, I'm thankful for it. "How about some ice cream?"

13

At the beginning of June, our school held a field day. Students competed in events like sack races, water balloon tosses, long jumps, and all sorts of athletic-seeming feats that were mostly designed to get us out of the classroom and hopefully having fun. But my friends and I were in it for the victory and bragging rights. Cru, Morris, and I signed up for the hundred-yard dash not only to win the plastic gold medal on a blue ribbon but also to figure out which of us was the fastest. I remember fueling up on oatmeal that morning, warming up and stretching, and running as fast as my legs could take me. I won gold, of course.

And today, hearing Grandpa offer an easy excuse to leave this house and its pushy ghost, I run faster than at field day. I probably set a world record.

Before Grandpa can put his baseball cap back on, I grab his hand, tug him though the backyard past Dad, Gus the plumber, and Mr. Morgan, and leap just beyond the fence. The second I pass the gate, Maxwell's hold over my arm begins to evaporate. I breathe a sigh of relief and take a few more steps away from the house, for good measure.

Grandpa smiles and adjusts his lopsided cap. He wears a pair of blue jeans with an old smudge of beige wall paint on the knee, but at least his mint-green palm-tree-print shirt looks neat and presentable. He's slightly out of breath at the burst of unexpected movement. "Wow, you must really love ice cream."

"You heading to the new gelato place?" Mr. Morgan asks. "They make an amazing fig-and-goat-cheese one. They're a commercial tenant of mine: mention I sent you and they'll give you a scoop on the house."

I don't know about fig-and-goat-cheese-flavored dessert, but I do like the idea of free ice cream. I'm about to thank him when Grandpa speaks first.

"Thanks, but that's a little fancy for me. I'm taking the boys to Culpepper's Creamery. Used to love Icky's, but that space is a wine-and-yoga place now."

Mr. Morgan nods and continues his conversation with Dad and Gus. He and Grandpa seemed friendly enough, but there was something underneath Grandpa's responses that I can't pin. He sounded polite but angry too. I don't know what it has to do with Mr. Morgan or gelato.

Leo, who wasn't part of my epic dash outside, finally jogs out to join us, a light sweater draped over his arm. "Can I get a cone this time, Grandpa?"

Grandpa snickers and ushers us away from the house. "A cone? You think my pension pays that much?" He barks out a laugh like Leo and I somehow understand retirement jokes. "You know the rules, kiddo. Standard cup it is. Cone on your birthday only."

He ruffles Leo's hair, and Leo laughs as he dodges away. My arm twitches oddly, despite us being totally off Warner Place property, and my eyes flick up to the attic. Maxwell watches us, his face no longer angry. The purse of his lips actually looks sadder this time.

I don't understand that kid. He's always some version of negative: sad, frustrated, probably gassy (if ghosts have working digestive systems). I don't think I've ever seen him genuinely smile.

Then again, as much as I like my alone time, I guess I'd be gloomy if that alone time lasted over four decades. No family, only vacationers, and bound to this house: what a miserable existence.

No excuse for trying to ruin *my* existence, though.

I brush off that pang of sympathy and focus instead on the other new, unwelcome realization: His power is growing stronger. Somehow, he was able to reach me even past the boundary of the fence. I gulp.

"Did I hear you're heading to Culpepper's?"

It takes me a moment to realize who is speaking. It's Ms. Anita, with her floppy gardening hat on, leaning over her back gate and smiling at us.

"Anita! It's been ages!" Grandpa strides over to her. He removes his hat and smooths down his hair. "Join us, won't you? I want to show my grandsons Sunnyside one last time before the move, and you're the pro at this end of town."

More company? I suppress a groan as Ms. Anita agrees. I like her, but I wanted to get away from the house as fast as possible without incurring my parents' wrath—they can't get mad if Grandpa invites me out, despite any sort of grounding. But this has turned into a whole social event.

It's hard to stay grumpy when the sun is shining, the cool ocean breeze is blowing, and a ghost isn't possessing your right arm. Grandpa, Ms. Anita, Leo, and I amble down the boardwalk toward Culpepper's. I scroll through my messages from Cru and Morris, trying not to get too envious of the late-night *Warricane* session they're planning.

Ms. Anita laughs at something Grandpa says, and he joins in. I look up from my phone. They're both smiling, and Ms. Anita lightly raps Grandpa's forearm before laughing again. My face scrunches instinctively. Are they flirting?

"I would've protected you," Grandpa says, his voice suddenly deep and noble. "My nickname in the navy was Valiant Vargas."

"Protect who from what?" I ask. Grandpa got winded from dashing through the backyard, and I don't think I've heard anyone anywhere use that nickname for him. I should probably discourage any riskier physical activity.

"Don't worry, Barnaby. Your grandfather is joking," Ms. Anita says, swatting Grandpa playfully on the arm again. "I was just telling him about this cutesy stuffed lamb doll my daughter bought for me. Get this: she swore the thing was possessed!"

I freeze my face to avoid looking too eager to talk about ghosts. "Possessed? What'd it do?"

"She said it bleated while she was driving. Can you imagine? A little doll with no battery-operated anything. My daughter turned her car right back around and demanded a refund from the secondhand shop owner!"

"So what do you think?" I ask carefully. Maybe Ms. Anita's experience can shed some light on what to do about my own situation.

"I think my daughter probably had some of her weird music on in the background and got confused."

I don't let it drop that easily. I turn to Grandpa. "Didn't Grandma Violet believe in all that supernatural stuff?"

"She did," Grandpa says. "But her scary ghost stories are from back in the Philippines. There aren't any ghosts *here*."

"How can you be sure?"

"Oh, Barnaby, I didn't mean to spook you. You don't have to worry about ghosts," Ms. Anita answers. "They don't exist. And besides, a possessed lamb doll—isn't that just the silliest thing you've ever heard?" Ms. Anita gives a dismissive wave that I'm sure she means to be reassuring.

"Bleating isn't that baa-d," Grandpa pipes in.

The two begin laughing again, and my stomach churns, partly from Grandpa's awful joke, and partly from the thought that they think this is silly. What I'm going through with Maxwell is the furthest thing from amusing, and their laughter makes it clear what they wouldn't be good allies against the supernatural. They'd be too busy flirting and giggling.

A heavy rumbling in the distance draws all our attention.

"What's that? Is a storm coming in?" my brother asks.

"No, I think it's those bulldozers at the Grand Seabird Hotel," I say. Ahead, the tall, once-stately resort stands drab on the hill, yellow-orange machinery lurking at its feet and creeping closer.

Ms. Anita and Grandpa sigh in unison.

"End of an era. I spent my high school summers as a pool attendant there," Ms. Anita says wistfully.

"Violet and I had our fortieth wedding anniversary dinner in the Grand Seabird ballroom," Grandpa says.

"I still have the phone numbers of my friends on the hotel staff in my address book. Haven't cracked that thing open in years."

They both go quiet, lost in memories too precious to share. A wrecking ball bursts through the east wall of the Grand Seabird, and dust, wood, and stone rain down. By the end of the day, those memories will be the only place the Grand Seabird Hotel stays standing.

"What are they going to build there?" Leo asks.

Grandpa adjusts his hat to shield his eyes from the sun. "Another hotel, I think. One of those boutique ones with no personality."

"Some of the new hotels are pretty cool, though," I counter. "We stayed at one in Los Angeles over spring break. A robot brought us fresh cookies in the lobby!"

Ms. Anita angles to look at me. "You think this new hotel will need a non-robot pool attendant? I'm pretty sure I can still balance a tray full of tropical drinks and club sandwiches," she says with a wink.

At this, Grandpa laughs, and the sadness emanating from him earlier ebbs like the tide.

I thought Grandpa was glad to be leaving Sunnyside behind. Since Grandma Violet died, he seemed so lonely and listless every time we called, and keeping up his house on his own was more trouble than he could manage. Yet now that we're here helping him pack, I'm not so sure that the sadness we saw on him necessarily meant he was done with the place.

Maybe he's just sad that the partner who stayed by his side for decades is gone. And maybe the answer my parents suggested—moving away from it all—isn't a solution to that. By the warm look on his face as he and Ms. Anita spin some wild tale of her using her motorized scooter to whip orders and hot towels around the pool, I wonder what a real solution might look like. I wonder if he even knows that himself.

14

We toddle back to Warner Place, our bellies full of chocolate ice cream. Mr. Morgan and Gus are gone. The hot tub bubbles brightly, and Dad is already lounging in it, "testing it out," he says.

"I take it the hot tub was an easy fix?" I ask Dad.

He's so relaxed he doesn't even open his eyes. "Yes, and you got so lucky, Barnaby. The hot tub itself wasn't damaged. Mr. Morgan was forgiving enough to not charge us extra for Gus's visit and the cleanup."

I search for evidence that Maxwell inflicted his ghost powers on anyone while we were gone, but everything looks intact. I exhale in relief. "So nothing else went wrong?"

One of Dad's eyes opens. "Why, were you expecting something to?"

"No, no, not at all! I'm just glad nothing else happened."

Dad's eyebrow rises at my vague statement. "And it won't happen again, right?"

I consider the best way to word this. "Right. I personally won't do anything to mess up our stay here." I make no promises for Maxwell and his behavior.

My careful answer appeases Dad, and that single eye shuts again.

Grandpa stays outside to chat with Ms. Anita while Leo and I head inside. Leo plops in front of the TV with Pao, and I ascend the stairs, bracing myself for another confrontation with Maxwell. Sure enough, he's waiting for me in the attic, his arms already crossed.

"Did you talk to Mr. Morgan?" I ask, shuffling over to my luggage for a clean shirt. Culpepper's Creamery was nice but sweltering, and a glop of chocolate ice cream dribbled down my shirt before I even took my first lick.

I expect an immediate "No way!" or some other angry sentiment, so I'm unnerved when I'm met with silence. I turn to face Maxwell. He's at the window now, staring out over the backyard.

I change my shirt. It does stink a little bit; Maxwell might be right about me needing to shower, but I'll never admit it. I go to join him. He's watching Grandpa and Ms. Anita with the same pensive look as when we left the house earlier.

"What's going on?" I ask.

"I—I know him," Maxwell says. His face crumples slightly, like his brain is struggling to grasp something that flutters right out of reach. "He and a woman used to walk down the boardwalk every day. She used to sing."

The mention of the woman hits me right in the chest. My grandmother. Did Maxwell know her?

"What song was it?" My question comes out quietly. I reach for a dirty sock I'd tossed on a chair nearby, just to keep my hands busy. This one stinks too.

"It wasn't only one song. She sang everything and anything. I recognized some disco music—she loved ABBA. But then she'd also make up songs about whatever was happening around them."

A memory of Grandma singing about string beans as she stirred a pot at the stove floats back to me. The kitchen air was humid from the soup and laced with the scents of onion and tamarind. I was Leo's age and sitting at their plastic-covered dining table, trying to put together the single, thousand-piece puzzle they had in the house. The puzzle was of a rose garden and took nearly the entire week we stayed with them.

Suddenly there's an ache in my chest, like a tight hug I can't wriggle out of, nor do I want to. I used to *like* coming here to Sunnyside. There was a time, not so long ago, when I didn't see our rare days here as a total waste of my summer.

Sunnyside feels empty without her. I can imagine it feels a whole lot emptier for Maxwell.

"That was my grandma Violet. She died last year." I wad the sock in my hand and toss it toward my suitcase. The sock overshoots it and slides farther away.

Maxwell steps back from the window. "Oh. I'm—I'm sorry. She seemed kind. For what it's worth, she was a much better singer than anyone who ever stayed here. I hate that karaoke machine downstairs."

I snicker, despite the ache. "Have you tried scaring them into stopping?"

Maxwell shrugs, and there's a restlessness in the way he begins to pace around the room. "Actually, I didn't always used to scare people. At first, I tried talking to the guests here. I sang along to a Prince song once—that didn't go well. Every time, people would run out and whine to Mr. Morgan. Then, the next day, there'd be some exorcist or holy person or spirit speaker in here trying to kick me out."

"Obviously they all failed, though. Like me and the pizza seasoning."

This time, Maxwell laughs. I scan the sound for any sense of evil-villain amusement, but it's a normal laugh. I think.

"Seriously, how could some oregano shoo me away?" Then Maxwell's face goes serious. "I wouldn't say they failed, though. The experts Mr. Morgan brought in didn't banish me, but they . . . they trapped me."

"Like in *Ghostbusters*? In that toaster-looking ghost trap?"

"Huh? I never got to see that movie! They played it at the theater on Main Street, but Dad never had time to go with me."

"We could watch it if it's on one of the streaming services downstairs. There's this part where—" I begin before realizing what I'm doing.

Am I actually inviting Maxwell to watch a movie with me? Somehow, I started seeing him less as a tricky ghost and more as a frustrated kid. I sympathize with him over all he's been through, but I'm still not sure I want a ghost hanging out with me for the next few weeks. I rush ahead before he takes me up on the offer.

"Anyway, in the movie, they trap the ghosts in the toaster thing, then put them in a more permanent jail at their fire station headquarters. You're still here, so I'm guessing none of Mr. Morgan's are ghostbusters like that."

"I guess not. When I say I was trapped, it was more than the usual being stuck somewhere on our property. It's like they disintegrated me, and I couldn't leave the attic in that form."

I raise my eyebrow. "Disintegrated? What does that even mean?"

"Well, you know how you actually see me in my human form right now?"

I nod.

"I just kind of existed as a cloud after the experts did their magic or experiments or whatever. It was like they turned me into those tiny dust particles that float in the air, the ones you only see when the sunlight hits them a certain way. I could see and hear everything. And"—he winces—"it hurt each time."

My eyes widen. "Wait, you feel pain? How does that work, if you don't even have a body?"

"I don't know. I actually don't feel much of anything. I don't get sick or hungry, but these attempts to banish me—that's the only time I've felt physical pain as a ghost. And I couldn't rematerialize for years after. So all that time I was stuck in here and I couldn't interact with anyone: no talking, no showing up in my human form to talk or scare or sing badly. Just watching everyone come and go, for years."

He kicks at the floor, but of course there's no sound. Now Maxwell's anger and his distrust of Mr. Morgan make sense. He was already alone before, after his parents moved out. Then because of Mr. Morgan's attempts to exorcise him, Maxwell spent years even more isolated in his own house.

"That sounds pretty awful."

The genuine sympathy that leaks into my voice seems to jar Maxwell. The look on his face reminds me of when Leo offered him some graphic novels. Maxwell doesn't seem used to anyone being kind to him. And as much as I want to be rid of him, that thought stings.

"I just want to figure out my unfinished business, whatever it is, and move on. If I could reach my family, they'd tell me what it is I'm missing."

"Ms. Anita!" I blurt out. The memory of her address book springs into my mind. I relay how we had walked by the Grand Seabird Hotel and she'd mentioned keeping everyone's contact information. Maybe that included Maxwell's parents.

Maxwell gives me the first sincere smile I've ever seen on him.

"Let's ask her now!" he says cheerily. He begins to go transparent, as if he's disappearing here to pop up right in front of Ms. Anita downstairs.

"Wait! You aren't going to ask her yourself, are you?"

"Why not? She's in the backyard with your grandfather. It looks like she's going home. We should go now!"

I sputter. "It's been forty years—you sure you want to spring that 'Hi, I'm the ghost of the kid next door' bit right this second?"

"She'll be happy to see me."

"Or terrified. I . . . I don't think it's a good idea."

"Fine. Then how about I ask through you?"

I step back. "That's definitely not a good idea!" No way I'm willingly offering myself up for ghost possession. When his face falls, I add, "This might scare her, that's all. She's in her late seventies, and she lives by herself. She doesn't believe in ghosts—she thinks it's all silly. So the thought of the house right next door being haunted might be too . . . much."

Maxwell finally nods. "Fine, fine. You do the asking. Can you go now?"

I peek out the window; thankfully, the opportunity has passed: Ms. Anita waves at my grandfather before pulling her back door closed.

Yuck. I do not want to get caught between those two while Cupid launches arrows. All the more reason to be glad we didn't dash down immediately.

"Tomorrow," I promise Maxwell. "I'll ask tomorrow."

15

I meet tomorrow far too soon.

I crack an eye open unwillingly. People chatter somewhere beneath my window so loudly they might as well be in the attic with me. From my comfy spot in the bed, I angle my head toward the seashell-shaped wall clock. It's a little after eight o' clock in the morning.

Who is even up this early?

I flop my head down onto the mattress and drag a pillow over my ears. The voices manage to sneak past the fabric and goose feathers and pummel my eardrums. No way I'm getting back to sleep with this racket.

With a groan, I tumble out of bed and trudge toward the window. I'd left it open last night, when it was blissfully quiet, to get some fresh ocean air and soothing wave noises. I scan the ground below to find who's guilty of waking a kid up early in the middle of summer.

To my surprise, it's Mr. Morgan. He's in a different blue business suit today, and he stands next to a petite brown woman wearing a magenta blazer with matching high heels and a white dress. The woman has the shiniest black hair I've ever seen and is snapping photos of the house with her latest-model phone. I sidestep slightly to make sure I'm out of the frame.

"People pay good money for these antique fixtures," she says. She raises her sunglasses to squint at something on the side of the house, then takes another picture.

"Then let's see what we can sell, Saiirah. No good any of this will do at the dump," Mr. Morgan says.

Then he lowers his voice—he chooses to do this now, after I've already woken up?—and points out a few more things. The way they're eyeing the house, like they're picking at it for parts, makes me uneasy.

I want to find out what they're saying. With a peek around the room to make sure Maxwell's not around, I pad downstairs. The office door is closed. Mom is probably already working, with Pao curled up next to her. The rest of the bedroom doors are closed too. It looks like I'm the only unlucky one who got woken up by a business meeting I wasn't invited to.

I creep over to the kitchen so that there's only a wall, a window, and a few potted plants separating me from

Saiirah and Mr. Morgan. I stay quiet and turn my ear to them.

"—are finalizing the terms of the deal now. We should hear back by the end of the week," Mr. Morgan says.

"Then I'll see if I can get my team out here to assess these fixtures. Anything inside worth looking at?"

The patio wood creaks like Saiirah is leaning to peek inside, and I flatten myself against the wall. Not that there's anything wrong with me walking around the house my family rented, but if they saw me, they'd stop talking business. And all this talk of money and dumps and deals seems important in a way I'm not quite sure of yet.

"Hmm," Saiirah says. "Can't see much. Mind if I go inside?"

I'm about to scramble over to the refrigerator to pretend I was here making breakfast when Mr. Morgan answers. "No, there are renters in there. They knew we'd be taking a look at the exterior this morning. I should give them more notice before entering, though."

I blow out a breath in relief, but it's premature: Maxwell suddenly blinks into view next to me. He glares out the window at Mr. Morgan and Saiirah.

"Who is that?" Maxwell asks, gesturing at Saiirah, who is now typing furiously on her phone.

"I don't know," I whisper. "I think she works with

Mr. Morgan. They were talking about selling fixtures, whatever those are. And she wanted to come inside, but we're here."

"Yes. We are."

I'd meant my family and me—the actual renters—but now does not seem the time to correct him, not with that offended gleam in his eye.

"I can't believe he wants to sell off parts of my family's house. None of this is his to sell. It's mine. I'm still here!"

"Well, on paper, it's his, unfortunately. I don't think courts really recognize the rights of ghosts."

Maxwell grumbles under his breath.

"The folks from Blue Spoon Betty's will be in town next Friday," Mr. Morgan says. "You can accompany them on the walk-through of the property and take a look at the interior."

I gasp aloud at the mention of Blue Spoon Betty's.

Maxwell's eyebrow rises. "Who is Blue Spoon Betty?"

"It's not really a who, it's a what: it's a bakery that sells warm cookies!"

"That's all? Warm cookies?"

"Oh, you don't understand, these are the best cookies ever! They're warm and gooey and the size of my hand. They're the most popular cookie bakeries in the state, with lines out the door every time they release a new flavor.

For my friend Cru's birthday, his aunt waited an hour to get him two dozen limited-edition blue velvet cookies for his party. I ate so many that when I went number two, it was the color of—"

"Whoa, stop right there! I don't need to know!" Maxwell's face twists in disgust.

"I'm just saying, they're a hugely successful bakery. And if they're scouting Sunnyside for a location, they're going to be the most popular thing on the boardwalk."

"Here," Maxwell says slowly. "The location they're scouting is . . . my home." He whispers the last word.

We both go quiet, and outside, Mr. Morgan and Saiirah have gone silent too, staring at their phones.

The deal Mr. Morgan was talking about: He's selling Maxwell's home to Blue Spoon Betty's. They're going to sell off anything of value in here, demolish the house, and put a trendy, soulless—but utterly delicious—cookie bakery in its place.

The look Maxwell gives me tugs at my heart, hard. "What would I do? What would become of me?"

"I—I don't know." How can he haunt his old bedroom if there isn't an old bedroom anymore? "I don't know how the whole ghost thing works."

"Me neither. I mean, I know I've been one for decades, but there isn't exactly a manual. You have to go talk to him."

"Now?"

"Why not? He's right there!"

"But then he'll know I was eavesdropping."

Maxwell huffs. "If you won't help . . ."

My right arm starts to tingle, and I look up at Maxwell with horror. "Stop that!"

Maxwell shakes his head. "Mr. Morgan won't listen to me, Barnaby. I need you to talk to him for me. Tell him he can't sell my house!"

"I get where you're coming from, but you have to stop messing with me like this!"

"I'm just trying to push you to hold up your end of the bargain! Oh no, they're starting to leave. You have to go, now!"

His voice rises to a shout with the last word, and suddenly the tingle in my right arm is replaced with a shot of energy in both arms. I'm unable to stop myself from opening the kitchen door. I dig in my heels, but Maxwell is clever. He uses my arms to latch onto the doorframe and slingshot me outside.

Mr. Morgan and Saiirah gawk at me in surprise.

Mr. Morgan smiles. "Good morning, Barnaby. How can we help you?"

If it wasn't weird enough that I was standing out here in my pajamas, I'm losing the fight with Maxwell over control of my arms. Which means that though my legs are firmly planted, my arms are swinging wildly around me.

They alternate between pointing at the house and reaching for Mr. Morgan.

Saiirah lowers her phone. "Young man, are you all right?"

"Yes, perfectly fine. Just, um, exercising!" I don't know what grand plan Maxwell had for this conversation, but I am not prepared to conduct real estate negotiations with Mr. Morgan on behalf of a ghost. Especially not when that ghost is coercing me like this.

One arm swings in such a wide circle that I'm nearly knocked off-balance. I need to get out of here. Ahead, past Mr. Morgan and Saiirah, the back gate is wide open. If I can make it onto the boardwalk, off this property, it'll strip Maxwell from me.

I take a deep breath. "I'm going to go for a run. Excuse me. And you might want to clear a bigger path. Sorry in advance."

Every word I said was both cryptic and incredibly rude, but it's an emergency. I channel all my energy into my legs and bolt toward the gate. I whip past Saiirah and Mr. Morgan so fast that Maxwell doesn't get a chance to pull any other stunts. As I fling myself out of the gate, his hold on me sputters . . . but he doesn't let go yet.

I have to run two more houses away before I regain full control of my body. Unnervingly, Maxwell was able to extend his control even further. He's getting more powerful, faster, in ways I can't even imagine. I can't let my guard down for a second: I may understand his hurt and frustration, but for now, it's still me or him. And I'm as determined as ever to not let this ghost ruin my summer.

Turning back toward the house, I walk to my next destination: Ms. Anita's.

16

Ms. Anita is already outside in the garden, bent over a low planter with a watering can in hand. I greet her, and she tilts up her head and smiles at me under the floppy brim of her straw hat.

"Barnaby, good morning to you too! You're up early."

"Don't I know it," I grumble.

I scan my limbs again for any trace of Maxwell's control, but either his reach doesn't extend to Ms. Anita's yard yet or he's given up. I let out a sigh of relief and return Ms. Anita's smile.

"Mr. Morgan was talking to someone right under the window of my room, and I—"

She straightens. "Where are my manners? Have you eaten yet? Take a seat," she says, not even waiting for a response. She waves at the wrought iron table and chairs nearby. "I don't suppose you drink coffee."

I shake my head. I doubt she'd let me get a word in, even if I tried.

"Sit tight. I'll fetch some tea. And I have some of Winston's croissants. He supplies the Cormorant Café. Have you been there yet?"

Another shake of my head.

She sets down her watering can and disappears inside her house, still chattering and asking questions that don't actually require answers.

For a moment, I consider retreating into the sleepy quiet of the rental house too, but I remind myself I came here for information. I also don't want to disappoint this nice, croissant-sharing neighbor. Besides, I'd rather be where Maxwell isn't.

I sit, as directed. There's something beautiful about this beach in the morning. I hate to admit there is a good side to being woken up early, but I haven't seen the beach this peaceful. The lifeguard camp hasn't assembled yet, and the sand is only dotted with a few people walking their dogs, a couple of joggers, and a man with a metal detector. Seagulls soar overhead, their calls clearer without any human chatter or music. Even the waves seem gentler and more sparkly, probably because they're not battling a bunch of selfie-taking, splashing tourists for territory on the sand.

Ms. Anita emerges a few minutes later with tea and a plate piled high with a dozen croissants. Something twinges in my chest. She lives by herself, and these pastries only stay fresh for a couple of days. Does Ms. Anita always buy this many, in case anyone drops by? I suddenly feel guilty that I didn't come with Dad to introduce myself when we first arrived.

"So Mr. Morgan is finally going through with the sale, hmm?" Ms. Anita says.

I take the teacup she offers. "Seems like it. He mentioned Blue Spoon Betty's."

Ms. Anita frowns. "He's been in negotiation with them for ages. I told him I didn't think it was a good idea, but he's already greased the city council wheels to turn that lot from residential to commercial."

I must look confused because she adds, "To knock down that house and put up a business instead."

"I hadn't thought about that. This whole part of the boardwalk is all houses. And everyone's okay with him just dropping a storefront in the middle of it?"

"Not everyone. This may be an unpopular opinion, but living next door to a commercial cookie bakery doesn't sound too lovely to me."

I sip at the tea and consider. "It would cut into the quiet of this place, that's for sure. Bakers have to get up really early, don't they?"

I think of Mom's short-lived obsession with sourdough and cake decorating a few years ago. Our television was always showing some reality-television baking competition.

"If they're about to change everything, why don't you just move away?" I ask.

"Why would I be the one to move? I was here first!" she says, with a snarkiness clearly meant for Mr. Morgan. It's exactly what Maxwell would say. "Besides, my house is on the historic register. It's protected and preserved as the home of the town's first female council member: my mother."

She beams with pride, and I'm suddenly hit with the reminder that I'm only a visitor here for a few short weeks, a tiny blip on the timeline of this community. Before I showed up, Sunnyside had a rich, vibrant history, and it'll do so long after we pack up Grandpa's house and leave.

"You must really love it here."

"We all do. But like you said, everything's changing. And I guess I'll just have to adapt like always."

I glance over my shoulder at Warner Place. Not everyone adapts. Some people, like Maxwell's family, leave. They may not hold the dreamy, delightful memories of this place that Ms. Anita does.

"The people who used to live there"—I point at our vacation house—"before Mr. Morgan bought it. You sounded like you knew where the Warners went."

A shadow of sadness passes over her face. "We kept in touch for a while after they left, but we eventually fell off."

"I'm sorry, I didn't mean to—"

"It's all right. I—I knew the Warners at the most tragic time in their lives. Their son's condition deteriorated so rapidly, we were helpless. He was biking down the boardwalk one day, then the next . . ."

"Do you know what the cause was?"

"To be honest, I don't. But what I do remember are the rumors. That boy's death didn't sit right with any of us. I told the police about the people who'd come in and out of the house in the days before: a lot of Gene's friends but also people I've never seen before, and this is a small town. As far as I know, though, nothing was done about it."

The hair on the back of my neck rises. Maxwell didn't mention anything about his death being suspicious. Then again, he only remembers waking up years later and his family being gone. Was there more to his death than he knows? What if his family didn't simply move away—what if they were scared off?

Ms. Anita sighs. "Anyway, there are no hard feelings on my part. I understand them not keeping in touch. It was probably difficult to maintain a friendship that kept reminding them of that painful time."

It's suddenly all the more important I find his family. They might be able to share more about what happened to him so we can figure out his unfinished business.

"Do you happen to have their phone number or anything? I need to reach them."

She sets down her teacup, like she's trying to figure out how much more to tell me.

"Those baseball cards I found." I hurry out the cover story I'd mentioned when we first met. "They probably belonged to their son. I think they'd appreciate them."

Her expression softens. "That's very sweet of you. I can share the last address and phone number I have for them."

Finally, a lead!

"Thank you so much. For the info and for the breakfast."

"My pleasure. Eat up; you're a growing boy."

You don't have to tell me twice to devour another buttery croissant.

She plants her hands on the arms of the chair and lifts herself to stand. "Now, let me get that address book."

17

Main Street is empty this early in the morning. Clock hands lazily tick over nine a.m., and bleary-eyed salespeople sort through their keys in front of stores. Empty soda cups and wrappers overflow the sidewalk trash cans. Even the city's custodial crews haven't made their way out here yet. Grandpa insisted we come early, though: early bird gets the worm, he said.

In this case, the worm is a toy. I tried to tell him toys aren't really my style anymore and that video games are more precious in terms of money and social capital. He didn't listen, which is why he, Leo, and I stand at the edge of the sidewalk in front of the tiny storefront of Sunnyside Games and Toys. The green paint and yellow window trim must have been vibrant and eye-catching at some point, but they've since faded and are peeling and flaking in places.

The yellow door opens, and the salesperson, a tall teenage boy with a mop of curly black hair, ushers us in with a barely concealed yawn. He greets us, pockets the keys, and retreats behind the cash register to stare at his phone.

"Anything under twenty dollars, boys," Grandpa announces. "My treat."

I don't have the heart to tell him that *Warricane* cost nearly three times that amount. I survey the model airplane kits and trading cards, but nothing grabs my interest.

"Wow, anything?" Leo cuts in, his eyes wide.

Grandpa nods, and Leo practically squeals.

Grandpa wanders over to the window display of stuffed animals that Mom had pointed out on our drive into Sunnyside, and Leo and I begin to comb the too-narrow aisles together.

"What are you going to get?" Leo asks me.

"Nothing, I think. I might be a little too old for all of this."

"Too old for gifts? No way," Leo says. "How about a puzzle? Or an action figure. We just walked by that comic book rack."

I gaze solemnly up at the cardboard cutouts of superheroes. I could get a toy, but it'd be a waste of Grandpa's money. He likely won't let me walk out of here with twenty dollars' worth of the gummy bear packs by the register either.

I join Grandpa at the front window. "I don't think I want any of these toys."

Grandpa simply nods. "You can add that money to the lunch fund, then. Get yourself a fancy milkshake if you want. There's a place around the corner that your grandmother and I always used to drop by for their chopped salads."

The mention of Grandma pinches both of us, even if we don't mention it aloud. I don't get Grandpa alone often—we're lucky for this one-on-one time today because my parents have a call with some real estate folks—so I steal this opportunity to get information.

We walk through the store at a snail's pace. "Grandpa, I've been meaning to ask you about the house we're staying in, Warner Place."

His pace somehow manages to slow even further. "What about it?"

"Did you know the Warners? I'm trying to track them down to return some baseball cards."

"No, I'm afraid we must've moved to Sunnyside after they left."

I deflate. I was hoping for a little more information about the couple before I called them out of nowhere to ask about their son.

Grandpa continues. "They weren't the first—or last—to leave, though. This whole town is so different than when your grandmother and I arrived."

"Isn't that a good thing? Maybe they'll get some new customers at stores like this," I offer.

The strained way Grandpa looks at me tells me that, no, that isn't in fact a good thing. "Of course it's nice to see new faces. But lately, the city council has been approving all sorts of projects that longtime Sunnysiders aren't thrilled about."

I think of Ms. Anita and Blue Spoon Betty's. "But they could just vote those councilmembers out if they don't like it."

"Yes, that's usually how these things go. But not in Sunnyside." Grandpa picks up an elephant stuffie—Grandma loved elephants—and gives it a squeeze. "We tend to have the same people running things from year to year. There's only been one new member elected in the past five years, and that's because the other guy retired to a dude ranch in the Midwest."

He sets down the stuffie and moves down the aisle. I trail him.

"I don't understand. At school, my friend Cru lost his student council race because people didn't like his idea of getting rid of recess in favor of nap time. Voting is that simple."

Grandpa snickers. "When you're older, you'll love the idea of midday naps. And you'll understand that elections aren't as simple as you think. There are a lot of other factors that go into who stays on the city council. The rest of us don't have enough money or power to influence it either way."

"You must be glad to be getting away from all this."

He answers me only by ruffling my hair, but I catch a hint of sadness in his smile. Grandpa reaches for a bracelet-making kit next, the kind with multicolor beads and elastic string. "You know, Jim Carn, the council president, has a granddaughter your age. Have you met her?"

I shake my head. "I haven't really gotten around town much." Nor have I wanted to.

"Ah, well, this reminded me of her. She made friendship bracelets last summer, sold them on the boardwalk for five dollars a pop." The happiness in his smile returns at this memory. I wonder if he and Grandma bought some.

Leo runs up behind us then, waving an action figure in the air. It's an astronaut in full space-walk gear. The clear shield on the helmet can be raised and lowered, and if you press a button on the back, it raises a miniature American flag.

"Grandpa, can I get this one? It's sixteen dollars, so with tax"—my brother is somehow the only nine-year-old to calculate sales tax—"it's under twenty!"

"Good choice, Leo, my boy," Grandpa says. Then he turns to me. "You sure you don't want to get something too?"

"I'm sure," I say, heading to the cash register with them. "I'm going to save it up for a milkshake at lunch, like you said. This store doesn't have anything I want."

Because what I want is to be ghost-free, and that's sadly not for sale at Sunnyside Games and Toys.

18

Calling strangers on the phone is one of my least favorite things to do, along with getting cavities filled at the dentist and taking pop quizzes. But apparently texting a landline is impossible.

So me sitting in the vacation-rental kitchen, the clunky blue plastic phone sitting between Leo and me, must prove my dedication to helping Maxwell.

I don't know if he sees it that way. He paces between the window and the refrigerator, as if he's too nervous to even watch me dial.

I press the speaker button on the phone as it rings, and the sound floods the room. I turn down the volume. After Grandpa brought us back from the toy store, he and Dad went to run errands, but Mom is upstairs. I'd hate for the racket to bring her running.

Maxwell stops in front of us. "What if they answer?"

I eye his translucent form. The anxiety practically radiates off him. "Isn't that what you want?"

"What will you say?"

"We have the list right here," Leo says. He slides a torn sheet of notebook paper past his new astronaut action figure and toward the ghost.

"And if they—"

"Calm down," I cut in. "No one's even answered yet."

He resumes his pacing but stays quiet.

The continued ringing makes all of us nervous. It's entirely possible the Warners don't live there anymore; even if they did, they might not be home or willing to chat with unknown callers who could be telemarketers. But I keep this to myself.

We start to fidget after the tenth ring. Even Pao, who was seated by Leo's feet, leaves the room.

"We can try again later," Leo suggests.

And because we're all looking for an easy way out of this awkward situation, both Maxwell and I agree. I hang up.

"There's another thing we can do while we wait," I say, taking my own phone out of my pocket. "We can do an online search for the phone number. Maybe it's linked to social media profiles or something, anything that could give us a lead on where your parents went."

Maxwell nods, but I'm certain he has no idea what I'm talking about.

Leo scoots his chair next to me to look over my shoulder. Glancing down at Ms. Anita's neat handwriting, I type out the Warners' last known phone number. Halfway down the page is a promising result.

"There! We got a hit," I announce. "The phone number has been associated with a J. Warner. Could that be Joyce?"

Suddenly, Maxwell is next to me too. "Yes! That must be Mom!"

"Hmm, no wonder they were hard to find. The rest of these listings show people's full first names. I wonder why your mom just went with her first initial."

That same unease from when Ms. Anita mentioned rumors around Maxwell's death creeps in. Sometimes, if people are hard to find, it's because they don't want to be found.

"Looks like that J. Warner text is a link," Leo says. He taps on it.

The next page loads with information about a few different J. Warners. We read through addresses of properties around the country, other names, and social media profiles that may or may not be Maxwell's mother. Some are obviously not her—too old, too young, or with a totally different first name like Jamal or Janine.

By page four of the results, my eyes start to glaze over. I yawn and continue to scroll, looking for someone who might be *the* Joyce Warner of Sunnyside. Then Maxwell gasps.

"Stop!" he says, panic in his voice. "Go up. What did that say?"

I scroll up, and my heart dives into my stomach as I read the title of the link I'd bypassed.

Couple killed in crash on 101—Santa Barbara Examiner, November 1991

I gulp. "I—I don't think we—"
"Open it," Maxwell says.

I hesitate. Maxwell could activate his ghost powers, take control of my hand, and click on the link anyway if he wanted to, but he doesn't. I click and then set the phone down on the table so he can read it. I go to the refrigerator for some juice, to get out of the way.

At the table, Maxwell hovers where I was sitting, and Leo squints to see my screen too.

"'A single-vehicle crash on Highway 101 killed Gene Robert Warner and Joyce Ann Warner (Jones) Thursday night, officials said,'" Leo reads slowly. "'Witnesses say that just before eleven p.m., the vehicle swerved suddenly and rolled down an embankment, stopping when it hit a tree.'"

The air feels too still, too quiet. It's like even the seagulls got the memo that this is a solemn moment. Maxwell reaches out to touch the phone, as if he wants to read more, but his hand goes straight through it. The sound that escapes him is half whimper, half growl.

He sniffles. "They're . . . they're dead." His shoulders slump. "They have been for a long time."

I set my glass down. "I'm sorry."

I step toward him, and his glassy eyes go wide, as if remembering that my brother and I are there. Then, without a word, he blinks out of sight.

Leo whips his head around. "Where did he go?"

I place my hand on my brother's shoulder. "I don't know. He must want to be alone."

"This is terrible, Barnaby. He was holding out hope his parents were out there all this time."

"And that they'd be able to tell him what he was doing before he died so he could figure out his unfinished business. But now . . ."

I trail off, the thoughts whirling around my brain too rapidly to form words.

A few days ago, I would've given anything for more time away from Maxwell. But the look on his face as my brother read the article reminded me that he was human. Like Leo and me, he had parents who loved him, a home he felt cozy in, favorite foods, and posters of his favorite movies on his bedroom wall. All of that is out of his reach forever.

Maxwell already told us he can still feel pain as a ghost. This latest blow must really hurt.

"Come on," I say to Leo. "Let's go check on him."

"You said he wants to be alone."

I frown. "I think four decades is a long enough time to be alone, don't you?"

When we reach the attic, Pao is already here. This time of day, she's usually in Mom's office, but she must've sensed Maxwell's sadness. She's lying on the rug, her head on her paws. Maxwell sits next to her, trying, and failing, to pet her.

He speaks first. "You guys probably think I'm being a big baby."

"Not at all," I say. Well, at least not for the reason related to his parents. He does have the temper of a hangry toddler.

"My parents have been dead for decades. It shouldn't hurt this much."

Leo goes to sit next to them on the floor and pets Pao for real. "It's okay. My mom says there's no right way to *feel*. We just do."

Maxwell raises an eyebrow. "What does that mean exactly?"

"I don't know," I say with a shrug. "My mom reads a lot of wellness magazines. She picks this stuff up from there. But my guess is that it means that it's okay for you to be sad, even if it doesn't feel like it makes sense."

He nods like he understands. He probably grasps this concept more than the idea of a reverse phone number search online.

"You must've really missed your parents for their loss to hurt this much," my brother says. "Our grandfather still leaves the room sometimes when we come across an old picture of him and Grandma. He blames the tears on allergies and the dust in his house, since he was always the messy one."

The mention of my grandfather sticks with me. He loved my grandma fiercely, and when she died, it hurt him so much that my parents had to step in to care for him. But I bet if you asked him, he'd say even that horrible pain was worth it, given all the years of joy. And if I asked Maxwell about his parents, he'd probably say the same, eventually. That's the trouble with your heart being an open door, though: at some point, someone will slam it shut, and it'll rattle the whole frame.

Maxwell sighs. "I didn't think I missed them that much, to be honest. I always thought of them as just being out for groceries or in the next room. And I think I'd always assumed I'd see them again. Now it's impossible, and I . . . I don't know what to do next."

"You keep trying to finish the unfinished," I say gently. "We'll figure out what's keeping you here, and we'll set you free."

"You're just saying that to get me off your back."

I give him a small smile. "Well, that too. But I do want to help you."

It's the first time I've said it in a way that I really, truly mean it. Some of the shadows lift off Maxwell's face, and though he stays quiet, he doesn't disappear again.

I lower myself onto the rug, patting Pao on the head. All of us—the brothers, the ghost, and the dog—sit on the floor of the attic, lost in thought, the afternoon sun making us drowsy.

I mull over what I said to Maxwell and, more importantly, what I didn't say. *I do want to help you. Because there may be no one else left who can.*

19

The next morning, we get ready to go to Grandpa's to help him pack. With much of the repairs and sales paperwork taken care of, Dad finished the emotionally heavy task of packing Grandma's belongings. He hadn't invited my brother and me—because of the dust, Grandpa said. Wouldn't want to aggravate anyone's allergies.

Now that most of Grandma's belongings are boxed, it's time for Leo and me to place dishware in Bubble Wrap and assemble cardboard boxes. Mom has taken the day off work to help too, and we're starting with a big pancake breakfast.

She slides one onto a plate and hands it to me. "Eat up, we're leaving in ten minutes."

I reach for the butter. "Why does everyone always tell me to eat up?"

"Because if it was left to you, you'd play video games instead and waste away," she says, serving Leo a pancake.

As if to show me up, Leo digs eagerly into his plain pancake. He's positioned his astronaut action figure to make it look like he's holding the maple syrup bottle. Even Pao sits patiently, tail wagging, expecting her own doggie-sized pancake.

Dad fills his water bottle at the refrigerator dispenser. "You'll need that energy to help me take apart Grandpa's furniture. He insists on bringing his desk, but it's not going to fit through the door as is." He shakes his head.

I'm finishing my fourth pancake when a knock at the front door grabs our attention.

"It's open," Dad calls to the front, and to my surprise, Mr. Morgan strolls in.

No business suit today, but he's still too formal for this town in his pink polo shirt tucked into neatly pressed khakis. Meanwhile, my dad and I are both in old T-shirts and swishy basketball shorts.

"Good morning," Mr. Morgan says with a wave of the rolled-up newspaper. "*Sunnyside Gazette* for you."

"Hi!" Leo chirps as the same time as I groan, "Oh no."

I barely escaped the property bounds without smacking Mr. Morgan during his last visit. If Maxwell finds out he's here, he's going to get me in huge trouble in front of my parents. I flatten my hands on the dining table, as if preparing for the inevitable tingling and takeover.

"Thanks," Dad says. "The *Gazette*'s horoscope is eerily accurate. I did have a dip in my cosmic energy on Monday, just like it had predicted."

"What's he doing here?" I mutter to Dad.

Mom gives me a warning glare that I know means *stop being rude.*

But Mr. Morgan must've heard me, because as he strolls farther into the kitchen, he says, "I'm taking few pictures of the fixtures for my associate. We received some good news yesterday: Our deal with Blue Spoon Betty's finally went through! The lawyers are double-checking some last things, but we expect to sign by the end of the week."

"Congratulations!" Mom and Dad say in unison.

"So we have to leave?" I ask.

Mr. Morgan shakes his head. "They'll honor our contract for the rest of your stay—I made sure of it. Their engineering team may drop by for some quick measurements and soil tests, but I'll give you plenty of notice so it doesn't affect your plans. You'll be the last vacation renters before—"

"Before this place gets demolished."

He picks up on the worry in my voice but doesn't seem to understand why it's there. "Yes. They're hoping to have their newest location of Blue Spoon Betty's up by the end of fall! Finally, some real growth in this town."

He, Mom, and Dad gleefully chatter about the business side of it while Leo and I exchange concerned looks over our pancakes.

"This changes things. I knew we only had two weeks left in Sunnyside to work on this unfinished business mystery, but I hoped that Maxwell could convince some other vacationers to help him later," I whisper to Leo. "We'll be the last ones, though. So if we don't solve this . . ."

"Then it's possible no one will, ever," Leo says. "When they demolish this house, Maxwell won't even have his attic to haunt. Everything, everywhere, and everyone he ever knew will be gone. And we'll be gone too, back home."

This timeline suddenly grew more urgent for Maxwell, which could in turn make things trickier for me. "This isn't good. He's having a really hard time, and it's already making him unpredictable. The only way I've stopped him from taking over my body is by promising we'll work on this unfinished business to free him. But who knows what he'll do now?"

The bite of pancake goes sour in my mouth. Mr. Morgan is outside in the backyard with Dad and Pao now, and thankfully, there's still no sign of Maxwell. But I think of the last time I played *Warricane* with Cru and

Morris. We got pinned by enemy aliens during a quest to retrieve a rare ship part. Things weren't looking good for us, and if our characters were killed, we'd respawn back at our home base and have to start the mission over again. Cru, Morris, and I decided to make one last, big stand. Starlight grenades in hand, we burst through the wall of aliens, intent on completing the mission before the aliens took us down. We didn't succeed, of course. But we caused a ton of damage to our in-game opponents.

The sale to Blue Spoon Betty's: This is Maxwell, pinned by enemy aliens. Who knows how far he'll go to save his home or free himself?

I only hope he doesn't take us down with him.

20

I dig my toes farther into the warm sand, wishing the sun would stay above the horizon a bit longer. I don't know how long I can avoid going back to the vacation rental.

We spent the day at Grandpa's, sorting out old clothes and adding to the donate pile. Then, as the afternoon wound down, I suggested we go out for pizza and even nudged Grandpa toward an after-dinner stroll along the boardwalk while the rest of my family returned to our house.

None of that is what I want to be doing, but it's loads better than telling a ghost that—surprise—I am his last hope in avoiding eternity in a corporate cookie shop.

So staying far from the house is the best way to avoid that feeling of doom—both his and mine, because he's

100 percent going to take this out on me. I found a spot far enough from the property line to be comfortable that Maxwell wasn't going to suddenly appear and take charge of my arms. It's close enough that my brother's high-pitched yell reaches me, though.

"Hey, Mom wants you to come inside," Leo calls from the backyard fence. He has his arms folded on top of it, and he looks like he's lived there his whole life.

"I, um, want to see the sunset," I lie.

I see him call over his shoulder, no doubt relaying my message to Mom; then he turns back to me. "She says you can see it just fine from the house with us."

There's no arguing that.

As slowly as I can, I rise from my seat in the sand. Dad waves as I approach. At the table on the patio, my parents share a fancy slice of cheesecake they bought at the corner store.

"You look like you're picking up a tan," Dad says cheerfully. "Summer vacation in Sunnyside suits you."

"I guess."

"You want some cheesecake? There's an extra slice in the refrigerator," Mom offers.

I'm not in any hurry to return indoors, but the promise of cheesecake is too good to resist.

"Get me a fork too, please!" Leo calls after me as I enter the kitchen.

Since everyone is outside, the lights in the house are off, and the setting sun lends a warm orange glow to everything. It looks cozy. For the first time, I could envision someone making a home here, and I can imagine how hard it would be to leave.

My sentimentality is cut short as I reach for the fridge handle only to have Maxwell appear between me and the appliance. My hand goes straight through his chest.

I gurgle in surprise. "Don't do that! You could've materialized literally anywhere else in the kitchen."

"Have you been avoiding me?" he asks, not in an accusatory way but in the way that someone is worried that their friend is upset.

Is that what we are? Friends?

No. I shake the question out of my head. He's using me to finish his unfinished business. To him, I'm a tool. And just because I'm starting to understand how hard it is to be a ghost—a phrase I never in a million years would've thought I'd use—that doesn't mean we're friends.

"I've been busy with my grandpa's move."

I open the refrigerator and pull out the clear box containing a massive slice of cheesecake, complete with a perfect dollop of whipped cream.

"You're hiding something," he says. His gaze grows intense as it meets mine. "Is it about the house? Mr. Morgan has been here an awful lot lately."

I stumble back, holding the cheesecake close to my chest. "Mr. Morgan is just checking on everything: being a good landlord."

Maxwell snorts. "Yeah, right. His family's owned this place for ages, and they never show up to be nice. Tell me. I know you know something."

"Oh no, mind reading isn't a ghost power, is it?" My back hits the counter behind me. I have nowhere to retreat.

"What do you think?" Maxwell says. He takes a step toward me, and we're practically toe to toe. He raises his fingers to his temples, like he's concentrating.

My mouth goes dry. I can't let him root around in my brain! He could find something he could use against me, like how I call the dog High Princess Siopao of the Fuzzy Four-Paws in private. "Stop! I'll tell you, just stay out of there."

He lowers his fingers.

"The sale to Blue Spoon Betty's is finally going through. They're going to sign everything soon, which means that once my family leaves, that's it. They're going to tear down the house and build a store. I'm sorry."

Maxwell's face falls. "I—I can't stay in a cookie bakery!"

"I know."

"I can't even eat!"

"I know!"

His hands ball into fists at his sides. "This can't be happening. I—I need to get out."

"But you can't go past the property line," I begin, until I realize that's not necessarily true anymore. He somehow had a hold over my arms even after I ran out of the gate the other day.

He must be remembering the same thing, because his face goes determined. "I have a theory I've been testing."

It's my turn to glare. "What?"

"These new ghost powers—I've been getting stronger," he says. He lifts his hands and stares at them. "You can tell, right? And if this keeps up, I'll be able to leave the property altogether, as long as I have a host."

The tingling starts in my fingers, and I almost drop the cheesecake. "A host? You—you can't! You can't *possess* me just so you can leave!"

Maxwell's face scrunches. "Hey, I don't want to live in your smelly body either! I want to be free of this world altogether. There's nothing for me here." His voice wavers with emotion. "But if you're unable to finish my unfinished business by the time your vacation is up, I'll have no choice. I am not staying in a bakery."

Energy surges through my arms and, to my horror, my feet. Maxwell is getting stronger: that's for sure. With my fingers out of my control, I drop the cheesecake. The container lands upside down, ruining that perfect dollop of whipped cream. I whimper.

I don't have another second to mourn the cheesecake, because suddenly I'm loping toward the patio where my family is.

"What are you doing?" I whisper harshly.

"Testing my theory!"

Maxwell doesn't even use my arms to open the door. He just pushes straight through; my face smacks against it.

At the *oof* that escapes me, my parents and Leo turn.

"Where's the cheesecake?" Mom asks.

I stumble forward unwillingly. "I—I'm not hungry after all."

Dad laughs. "That's the first time I've ever heard you say that about cheesecake."

My legs carry me haltingly toward the back gate. Maxwell hasn't nailed down the art of literally walking in someone else's shoes. I must look as a coordinated as a newborn giraffe. But how I look is the least of my worries right now: Maxwell is going to practice leaving the property. In front of my parents.

I still have control over my head, which I swivel so I can meet Leo's eyes. *Maxwell!* I mouth, and my brother's jaw drops when he realizes what's happening. He jumps to his feet.

Suddenly, I'm at the back gate, my fingers fumbling clumsily with the latch.

"Barnaby, the sun's going down. Where do you think you're going?" Dad says.

"I—I want to go for a walk. You know, to, um, make the most of our time in Sunnyside." I hope the lie is believable.

"I'll come with you!" Leo says, scampering over.

I almost breathe out a sigh of relief. My parents might argue with me going for a stroll by myself, but if it's with my brother, then it's bonding time. Still, Mom raises an eyebrow. She looks like she's going to naysay the whole thing when another surge of energy zaps through my arms.

I glance down to see what's happened. My arms are suddenly wrapped around my brother.

I'm *hugging* him. This ghost is making me *hug* my brother. How dare he!

Mom's eyes go glassy as she coos a babyish "Aww! My sweet boys!"

I try to smile to make these actions seem more believable, but I'm pretty sure my face is set in a wide-mouthed grimace.

"Let's go. Now," I grumble in a low voice to both Leo and Maxwell.

We stumble away from Warner Place. We head past Ms. Anita's house toward Fern's Grocery, and I wait for my limbs to come back under my control. My heartbeat races as I realize that Maxwell's control isn't waning as quickly as I'd like. We're over halfway to the grocery store when my feet plant on the ground.

Leo stops too. "What's happening?"

His face pales, like he's seen a monster. I turn my head to peek at what he's looking at, and sure enough, Maxwell's own head is floating out of my shoulder.

"Nope!" I screech. "We're not doing this. Two heads are not better than one. Get out of here!"

If I could bat away his ghost head, I would. But his grasp over my limbs stays firm.

"I'm taking this body for a test drive," Maxwell explains to Leo. "This seems to be as far as I can get from the house right now. I tried leaving this body earlier, but it's like the house lassos me back."

At Leo's confused face, I heave a sigh. "Maxwell is planning to come with us if we don't finish his unfinished business before they tear down the house."

Leo gasps. "But we don't know what your business is yet!"

"No, no you don't," Maxwell says with a huff.

And we're not any closer without his family to clue us in. I purse my lips. In the distance sits the rubble of the Grand Seabird Hotel. That's what will become of Maxwell's home too, unless . . .

"We stop the sale!" I announce. "If we can convince Mr. Morgan not to go through with selling to Blue Spoon Betty's, you can stay at Warner Place the way it is. Then it's just a matter of waiting for a vacation renter who can help you and, to be honest, is probably way better at this unfinished business solving than I am."

"You really think you can do that?" Maxwell asks, skepticism threading his voice.

"It's worth a try," I say. "We'll have to build a solid case against tearing down the house."

The ideas fly so fast through my head that, for the first time all day, I see a path forward.

Maxwell must sense the change, because his hold on me suddenly wavers. I wiggle my toes on my own. "All right. Try. But you have to keep helping me with my unfinished business, okay? Or else I'll—"

"You'll possess my stinky body, I know. I'll help. But no more of this practice possession stuff, okay?"

"Deal."

"Um, can we go home now? People are starting to look at us funny," Leo says. "Can they see you, Maxwell?"

Maxwell's floating head shakes. "No. I'm purposely not trying to show myself since I'm using a ton of energy just to hold on to Barnaby. It's like the difference between a whisper and a shout. I can whisper to you two, but it takes more to shout out to the world."

"Great," I mumble. "So only Leo and I get the joy of dealing with you."

Sure enough, an elderly couple moves to the far edge of the boardwalk and speed-walks past, as if I might suddenly leap at them and scream "Boo!"

"Let's get back to the house. I've had enough of being a test subject for today," I say. "Maxwell, you doing the work, or should I?"

"I'm pretty tired from the walk, so I'm just going to let the house lasso me back. See you there!"

The ghost leaves my body, and I stretch out my arms to make sure they're truly mine again. Not that I want Maxwell possessing me, but he could've at least saved me the exercise.

"Lazy ghost," I mutter.

21

On a Monday morning, the dog park patrons are mostly other vacationers and a few people in businessy-looking wear, though none as formal as Mr. Morgan. The park is a fenced-in patch of packed dirt, flattened grass, and a couple of wooden benches. The benches are already occupied by three men laughing too loudly and clearly here to socialize as much as their dogs are.

"Come on, High Princess Siopao, let's at least make it a few steps in," I urge Pao.

Pao and I stay to ourselves just inside the chain-link fence, by the gate. I figured that after being cooped up with Mom all week, she could use the opportunity to stretch her legs. She's sweet on our morning walks, but this is the first time we've stopped at the dog park, and she is fighting me every paw of the way.

I had to pick her up and deposit her inside the enclosed

park. Then she planted her paws and refused to stray too far from the exit or engage with the other dogs.

I remove her leash. "Go ahead."

Pao huffs and stays put. She's one of the smaller animals here. At the far corner, two golden retrievers chase each other, and there's a sniff-happy Yorkie terrorizing a few dachshunds and a Lapponian herder wearing a Star Wars bandanna.

I squat down and pet her head. "Don't you want to meet any of your beloved subjects?"

She watches the golden retrievers, one now on its back and pawing at the air, and moves closer to me. I'll take that as a no.

A teen girl on her way out of the park with her German shepherd puppy stops to smile at Pao. She tucks a long, curly strand of purple hair behind her ear. "Why, hello there! Aren't you a cutie?"

Most dogs would love this attention. But Pao shrinks back against my leg.

Then the German shepherd puppy bounds closer, wanting to play. And Pao barks—*at a puppy*. The human equivalent would be my dad yelling at a Girl Scout offering him a cookie sample.

I apologize, but the damage is done. The girl scoops up her puppy, gives me an awkward *It's okay* wave, then dashes away.

I sigh. "No new friends, hmm?"

Pao pushes her furry face against my leg, like she'd rather stare at the weave of my jeans than make eye contact with anyone. The dog park was worth a shot, to get Pao out of her shell. But I get it. We're only here for a couple more weeks anyway. No point in forcing her to befriend some overactive puppies.

I move to reattach the leash to her collar when a pair of brown leather ballet flats stops near me. The owner of the shoes and the knee-high, gray-haired dog next to them is a tall white woman about my mom's age. She has kind blue eyes that match the flowers on her shirt.

I can't help the tiny prickle of annoyance. Did she not just see Pao snap at a puppy? We want to be left alone.

"First time in Sunnyside?" the woman asks.

I stand. "No, but first time at this dog park. Um, a quick warning: High—I mean, Pao here—doesn't really get along with other dogs. She mainly sticks around people she knows."

Right as I say this, the woman's dog goes to sniff Pao.

To her credit, the woman utters a low "Bertie," which sounds like someone warning a kid to be careful.

I stiffen and brace for Pao to bark or run behind me, but to my surprise, she stays where she is, cautious but calm. The other dog is wholly unlike the in-your-face German shepherd, and Pao seems to appreciate whatever this version of doggy politeness is.

"This is Bertrand, the unofficial doggy ambassador of Sunnyside," the woman says with a warm smile. "Got him from the shelter when he was a puppy. Took some time, but he's a friendly, gentle soul these days. He makes it a point to greet every new furry companion who drops by this park."

Surprise gives way to a tiny sense of betrayal. Pao's supposed to be a lone wolf—well, lone Maltese—in Sunnyside, like me. But now she's voluntarily interacting with another dog. She might make a friend here before I do. Then Pao does the unthinkable: she actually steps away from the exit and follows Bertrand a few steps farther into the park.

Abandoned, I'm forced to respond to Bertrand's owner. "Bertrand is good at what he does."

The emotional conflict must be plain on my face because the woman laughs. "Hi, I'm Serenity. I'm a pharmacist over on the east side, but I also work for the city. So I guess I'm an unofficial human ambassador of Sunnyside too."

I laugh and introduce myself. We watch our dogs trot around the enclosed space, and I swear it's like Bernard is actually telling Pao about the town because she's following him closely, ears at attention. Serenity asks what I like best about Sunnyside and gives me recommendations for more ice-cream flavors to try at Culpepper's, and I mainly nod and try to remain polite.

Then the peaceful morning quiet—well, other than playful barks of dogs—is broken by faraway clangs and rumbles. Serenity's mouth droops into a frown.

"That must be from the Grand Seabird," she says. "This place is changing so much, day by day."

I catch a hint of sadness in her voice, similar to the tone Grandpa took when talking about the town. "Wouldn't a new hotel be good for business?"

"Yes, but I can still miss the Grand Seabird. I can't picture the shoreline without it. That hotel always used to have the best Fourth of July fireworks display."

She sounds like Maxwell, all nostalgia.

"Are there going to be fireworks this year?"

"No, I don't think so. Bad for vacationers, good for the dogs, I guess."

I smile. "Pao will be thrilled with a non-fireworks holiday for sure."

"Here's a tip from a lifetime Sunnysider for you," Serenity says, her voice brightening. "Stake out your Fourth of July parade spot early. This may seem like a quiet town, but everyone sure comes out to Main Street for the celebration. Show up after ten a.m. and you'd better be six feet tall or prepared to stand on the tips of your toes for an hour."

"Thanks. I'm not planning on growing a foot this week"—unless Maxwell's ghost powers can make that happen somehow—"so morning stakeout it is. My little brother loves parades."

Serenity checks her phone and calls Bertrand over.

"We've got to get going," she says to me. "It was nice meeting you, Barnaby. In case I don't catch you at the dog park again, have a great rest of your time here."

A great time? Unlikely. But I thank her anyway, then call Pao over as they leave. Pao's white paws are brown with dirt, and a few dried leaves are stuck to her back from where she rolled around. I don't think I've ever seen her roll around on the ground—on my parents' fluffy comforter? Yes. On the dirt? No.

I attach her leash and ruffle the fur on her head. "Good job today, Pao." I swear she actually smiles at me. High Princess Siopao of the Fuzzy Four-Paws, beacon of solitude, actually made a vacation friend.

I guess old dogs *can* learn new tricks.

22

I lean against the doorframe of the office while Mom checks that her laptop microphone is muted.

"The library and back only, okay?" Mom says.

She's stuck on a video conference call all afternoon, so I had to time my interruption perfectly before I knocked to ask if Leo and I could go out. Dad left for Grandpa's early this morning. He asked the rest of us to take the day off from packing duty because of the electricians working on Grandpa's house.

Mom bets that Dad accidentally broke something important and is trying to clean up the damage before we see.

Either way, sitting around Warner Place seems like a waste of time, not only because of the investigation but because it's summer. Cru and Morris texted to ask if I could join them for *Warricane*, but Mom's important meeting hogs the internet connection. I gave up after it took five minutes for the game to even log in.

So when Leo mentioned an outing to the library, I agreed. Leo grabbed his roll of quarters for the book sale rack and a sweater, of course, and I tucked my phone in my back pocket.

"Not even a stop for a snack?" I ask Mom. "Culpepper's is a block over from the library."

"Fine. But no filling up on ice cream, and be back in time for lunch." Mom returns her attention to her laptop.

I leave the door slightly ajar for Pao to come and go. From her spot near the desk, Pao raises her head to look at me but seems to decide against joining us.

I tiptoe over to where my brother stands at the door of his room. "Let's go."

Leo follows me to the stairs, then pauses before descending. "Wait, are we really going to get ice cream? Because I'll need to go get the rest of my cash too."

"You have cash?"

"I save up my birthday money. Don't you?"

Mine goes straight to funding my video games. How else could I have gotten *Warricane* the day it came out?

"Um, sure," I dodge. "But I don't know if we'll have time for a Culpepper's stop, especially with Mom's strict lunch timeline."

"I think we will. The library's pretty small."

A small smile creeps onto my face. "Well, the library is only one of the places on our schedule today. I have an idea for another stop to make first."

Culpepper's Creamery is right next door to Morgan and Morgan Property Solutions.

I lead the way to the Morgans' office, but as we near, a familiar voice barking out of the Cormorant Café stops us. Sure enough, Mr. Morgan himself looms at the front of the line. He already has a paper cup in hand.

"—make it again," he says. The annoyance in his voice is clear to even Leo and me, who just walked in. "Or I'll buy this place next and fire you first."

I recognize the barista, despite the forced smile contorting her face. It's the teen girl with the German shepherd puppy that Pao snapped at. Her purple-streaked wavy brown hair is pulled into a low ponytail. A plastic name tag reading *Eleanor* is pinned onto her black cloth apron.

"Yes, sir," Eleanor says. She takes the paper cup from Mr. Morgan, and as soon as she turns around, the smile drops.

Mr. Morgan steps away from the counter and seats himself alone at a barstool by the open window. A couple who was heading to the barstools near him change direction and cram into a tiny leather booth instead.

"It's go time," I say to Leo. I try to channel the same

amount of confidence I have before starting a tough mission in *Warricane*. We flank Mr. Morgan, claiming the stools on either side of him.

He glances up from his phone, shocked to see us. Then his practiced, friendly demeanor slides on. "Hi, boys, what brings you out here? I hope not the coffee. Stunts your growth."

He laughs to himself as if he expects us to join him, which we don't.

"We saw you through the window and wanted to say hello," Leo says. My brother's voice is so earnest and pure that people instantly believe him. It's a superpower that he doesn't quite know he has, but I notice every time he escapes a grounding.

Mr. Morgan smiles for real. "Have you been enjoying Sunnyside? Has anyone told you about the big Fourth of July parade? I think it's mentioned in the welcome binder."

"Yes, but that's not what we're here about," I pipe up.

His face freezes in place, and I can tell he's already trying to figure out what I'm going to say so he can leap a step ahead of me. I didn't quite notice these shrewd businessman traits of his before, but I see now why Maxwell is wary of him. Maxwell has had years of observing Mr. Morgan at work.

"We heard what you told my parents, about us being

the last renters at Warner Place. Have you thought about, um, not selling to Blue Spoon Betty's?" I say.

He relaxes, and a low chuckle escapes him. "That's what this is about? I thought you did something to the hot tub again. What, you don't like cookies, kid?"

"I love cookies. But the house: it's been there for ages, and it sounds like you do get a ton of vacation renters."

Mr. Morgan drums his fingers on the table. "I do. It's usually booked way ahead in the year. The only way your dad was able to secure the three-week rental period is because I didn't want to juggle a bunch of reservations while handling this big Blue Spoon Betty's deal."

"So if it's booked pretty consistently, then there's no reason to cut off that stream of income, right?" I stole some of that language from Mom's speakerphone calls.

He chuckles again, but it sounds less like amusement and more like him buying time to think. "This is a pretty admirable hobby for little boys: real estate investment."

"We're not little," I say. How is twelve little? I'm as tall as my mom. "I just think that you should keep the house and not tear it down. You have plenty of properties around Sunnyside, right? Can't Blue Spoon Betty's take one of those, instead of one with an ocean view?"

"It's that boardwalk foot traffic they're paying for, kiddo. Once we get the contract signed and the final zoning change approvals from the city council, there won't be a single person strolling on the Sunnyside boardwalk without a cookie in hand."

I lock eyes with my brother, hoping he has some ideas. I only researched so much on the business side. I don't understand the deeper reasoning behind some of the points I'd made, but they sounded smart when I said them. Now I'm all out of points.

Leo takes up the charge. "Not if the town's angry at you. Everyone seems pretty upset about the Grand Seabird Hotel getting destroyed."

This actually makes Mr. Morgan pause. Again, I have no idea when my little brother became smarter than me, but I'm becoming more okay with it every day.

"Some people in this town want everything to stay the same forever, even if it stands in the way of progress."

And by *progress*, Mr. Morgan clearly means *money*.

"I think my coffee is ready, boys. Pleasure talking with you," he says, pushing his barstool back.

"Wait," I say. I hop off my stool and follow him to the counter.

He swipes his cup from Eleanor without so much as a thank-you, then stares down at me.

I try one last time. "Please, Mr. Morgan. Don't let them tear down Warner Place."

Mr. Morgan leans toward me. "You two are on my last nerve, kiddo. First the hot tub, now this whole save-the-house bit? I'm selling it: that's the end of the story. Stay out of my business." He straightens and slicks back a strand of glossy hair that has fallen out of place. "This whole conversation is a perfect example of why I don't want to deal with renters anymore."

He marches out of the Cormorant Café before Leo and I can respond. I watch him, a mix of hopelessness and anger churning in my stomach. Even ice cream won't be able to settle it.

Mr. Morgan had seemed reasonable the few times he met us at Warner Place. But that was all fake. The business suits in the beachy summer should've been a hint: He is money-driven. If there's a profit to be made, what good is preserving a century-old house that's seen the town of Sunnyside rise up from the sand?

"What a jerk," a voice says behind me.

I turn. It's Eleanor. She glares out the door Mr. Morgan exited through.

"Is he always like this? The fake-nice thing," Leo asks.

Eleanor leans forward, planting her elbows on the counter. "Yes, he is. My mother says he and his family have been ruining the town block by block since before I was born. And they get away with it because they wine and dine all those old men in city hall."

That must be what Grandpa meant about the other factors that go into who stays on the city council.

Then Eleanor shrugs. "That's how the world works, I guess. Things stay cute until people need cash."

My shoulders slump. "What a tough reality."

"We fight back the best we can," Eleanor says. Then she winks at me. "That triple-shot hazelnut cappuccino with two-percent milk he made me redo? I swapped it out for decaf."

23

As threatened, the Blue Spoon Betty's engineering team arrives Thursday morning. I don't know why I expected them in chef hats and aprons. The man and woman from Blue Spoon Betty's don boring blue collared shirts and clutch boring brown clipboards.

They lurk outside the house, talking to themselves so low I can't hear a thing. I station myself at the kitchen table to watch. Curse my inability to lip-read.

"What time are we going to Grandpa's?" Leo asks next to me.

Dad waits impatiently at the coffee maker. "After my first cup," he says. "I could've sworn I scheduled it to brew this morning. I remember the white indicator light and everything."

I'm not entirely sure if it's Dad's fault or if it's one of

Maxwell's pranks. Either way, an uncaffeinated Dad moves sloth slowly, so we have some time before we get into the car.

Leo lowers his volume. "What do you think those Blue Spoon Betty people are talking about?"

I shrug. "Probably business stuff, like how many parking spots they need."

When I turn to my brother, I jump at the sight of Maxwell next to him. Part of our deal was that Maxwell wouldn't mess with my family. What if my dad sees him somehow? How would I explain that I'm helping a ghost haunting our vacation rental without my parents blaming it on video games or the internet or too much sugar?

"Adult! Right there!" I whisper harshly. "He might see you!"

Maxwell isn't nearly as concerned as I am. "Relax. I'm only showing to you and Leo. Besides, your dad is fixated on that coffee maker." He points to the backyard. "Who are the clipboard holders?"

"The buyer's engineering team."

When we'd reported back to Maxwell that Mr. Morgan had not only refused to cancel the sale but that he was downright rude about it, Maxwell had simply sighed. This behavior seemed totally in line with what Maxwell had come to know about Mr. Morgan.

"And who is that?"

I follow his gaze to where the engineers have paused to address someone standing outside the gate. The young man in a brown shirt, a brown ball cap, and neon-green over-the-ear headphones juggles a stack of packages. He hands the engineers a sunflower-yellow box. It's tied with a white ribbon dotted with blue anchors. With a smile, the woman takes it and deposits the box by their bags before she and her partner continue working.

"Looks like a delivery person," I say.

Leo squints in their direction. "Wait. Do you think that yellow box is for us? Did those engineers just swipe our package? Blue Spoon Betty's is a porch pirate!"

The response comes from a source I don't expect, with a sureness I wouldn't have imagined. "It's for them. From Mr. Morgan."

Across the kitchen, there's a clatter as Dad roots around the cabinet for a mug. We can't have this conversation here. Dad may not be able to see Maxwell, but he can sure hear Leo and me.

"Follow me," I say quietly.

I lead Leo and Maxwell up into the attic so we can spy on the engineers.

"You sounded pretty certain that it was from Mr. Morgan. How do you know?" I ask. Using my phone, I zoom in on the yellow box and snap a photo so I can read the label.

For a split second, Maxwell's image flickers, like he's getting pulled into that other, 1980s reality he inhabits. "That yellow box, that ribbon . . . it's Mr. Morgan's mother's famous lavender sea salt shortbread. Mrs. Morgan is an avid gardener. She always uses homegrown lavender. The Morgans would give out those shortbread boxes to employees as thank-you gifts and during the holidays."

I lean against the window frame and analyze Maxwell's face. "You said *employees*. You mentioned your families had history, but your parents—did they work for the Morgan family?"

Maxwell nods. "My dad did. The Morgan family was responsible for the big boom in Sunnyside real estate development back then. My dad was on the construction crew for a lot of their projects. He tried to get a union started, but that must've fallen off after I . . ."

He doesn't say *died*, but Leo and I exchange a look anyway. Something about this intertwining with the Morgan family doesn't sit well. I can't help but feel like someone has mixed up the puzzle pieces so much we can't see the whole picture.

"What's a union?" Leo asks. He sits at the edge of the bed, next to my wadded-up blanket.

"It's when a group of workers band together for a cause, like better working conditions," I explain. "Remember that podcast Dad played on the drive here? About how a lot of Hollywood writers and actors went on strike—I mean, refused to work until there was better pay and health care and all that?"

Leo blushes. "Um . . . I . . . fell asleep. It was a long car ride!"

Meanwhile, Maxwell asks, "Wait, what's a podcast?"

I sigh. One thing at a time. "The main point is that Maxwell's dad was trying to get a bunch of workers together to ask for stuff from their bosses, the Morgans."

"That's right. My dad and his friends wanted better health benefits and actual breaks," Maxwell added. "One of their buddies got hurt on the job. He couldn't work after that, even had to quit their Wednesday-night bowling league. Dad said it inspired them to demand things that would prevent that kind of accident from ever happening again."

My brother taps his chin. "That sounds reasonable. But why would the workers have to fight for safety measures? Wouldn't bosses want their people safe?"

"More pay, more safety equipment, more time off: those cost money. Rich people don't really like parting with their money, even—and especially—if they have a ton of it," Maxwell responds, his face grim.

I shrug. "I guess that's how they got that money in the first place. I take it the Morgans didn't love that your dad was stirring up trouble for them?"

"Clyde Morgan—Mr. Morgan's father—and a few of his executives came over a handful of times to have serious conversations with Dad. They didn't want him organizing everyone and stirring up trouble, like you said. My parents had me stay in the attic while they talked business, but I could hear them get loud. Mom was saving to buy me a new boom box for Christmas, to play music to cover up the racket they made."

"So you have a bunch of reasons to dislike Mr. Morgan," Leo says. He tucks his legs underneath him and leans forward, as if he's ready to pick up some juicy secrets.

"And the Morgans have a bunch of reasons to dislike your family," I point out.

Maxwell rubs the back of his neck and floats away from the window. "Yeah, but it couldn't have been that bad. They didn't fire my dad or his friends. And they even gave us one of those yellow boxes during the holidays. I got to it first. My parents forgot I had a half day at school, and my dad rushed over at his lunch break to drive me home. He had the Morgans' shortbread box with him, and he made me bring it inside before he sped back to work." The wistfulness on his face fades into something sadder. "I thought my parents would be so angry I ate the whole thing, but then I—"

"Wait, holidays? This was in December?" I cut in. "You said you died in December."

"Yes, I did. So?"

The unease in my chest begins to roil like a storm cloud. The timing, the box of shortbread, the soured relationship between the Warners and the Morgans, the union, Ms. Anita's wariness, the neighborhood rumors: It's all coming together. And the paths running between each piece are too clean and clear for any of this to be coincidence.

"Barnaby, are you okay?" my brother asks.

I must have been silent for a while, because Maxwell and Leo are both staring at me.

"Maxwell, I know we were hoping your family would clue us in on what was going on when you died. But I think we might have figured out something big without them," I say slowly. "December 1984. You said you got sick, then died."

He nods.

I draw in a breath to steel myself for what I'm about to say. "I don't think you just got sick and died, Maxwell. I think you were poisoned."

24

Maxwell's entire image goes dark, as if he's more shadow than ghost. "Poisoned? No, that can't be right. I would remember if someone was out to get me . . . wouldn't I?"

I stay rooted by the window. "You said yourself that the moments around your death are fuzzy. Think about it. You're starting to put it together too, aren't you? Your dad was causing huge trouble for the Morgans, and they . . . well . . . they did something about it."

Maxwell tears his gaze away from me. He begins to pace around the attic. "It makes so much sense. I couldn't see it before. I didn't remember that yellow box until now. The Morgans must have done something to the shortbread. They *must* have poisoned me."

Leo slides off the bed. "They gifted a tainted box to

your family for the holidays? That's next-level evil. If you hadn't eaten all of it, your parents might've—"

"Wait," I cut in. "That means it's possible the Morgans didn't intend to poison *you*. Their beef was against your dad. They gave him the box at work, right? They didn't know your dad would pick you up at school early—your dad didn't even know it was a half day. The Morgans probably assumed he was going to break open the box and eat some before he got home."

Maxwell stops his pacing and casts a glare at me. "You know, it doesn't make me feel any better to know that they were trying to get my dad and not me. Accidental death is still death."

"I'm just saying, it's possible they didn't mean to kill you or anyone. Whatever they snuck into that shortbread, maybe they were just trying to get your dad a little sick, make him miss work or something."

Maxwell's eyes widen. "You know, he was worried about some big union election scheduled before work paused for the holiday. I could hear Mom constantly telling him to go to bed." He bit his lip in thought. "The Morgans might've been trying to keep him from voting to form a union."

"Your dad must have really been onto something if the Morgans were out to scare him like that," Leo says.

"Well, it worked, didn't it? After I died, my parents moved away from Sunnyside altogether and the Morgans got to build whatever they wanted, however they wanted." He slouches. "And I'll never get to learn how much my parents actually knew. Was it the grief that drove them away? Or were they scared? Did anyone realize what the Morgans had done?"

I zip my lips. We may be trying to untangle this mystery, but some questions are too tough for us to answer. Decades' worth of distance separate us from the truth, and whatever information his parents had, they took it with them to their graves.

Maxwell drags his hands through his hair. The move should've made his hair stick out every which way, but it flickers back into the shape I'm used to. He's going to look that way forever, unless we do something about it.

The air in the attic begins to feel too warm and stale. It's like even the house is begging us to go out there and fix this.

I clear my throat. "We need to figure out what this means for your unfinished business."

"I'll tell you what it means," Maxwell says, his voice serious. He drifts over to the window, between Leo and me, and stares outside. "It means I know what I have to do to free myself from this world so I can finally join my family: We need to avenge my murder. We need to punish Mr. Morgan. That's what my unfinished business is, Barnaby. And you're going to help me with it, like you promised."

I go cold. This isn't what I'd signed up for. "Punish? We don't know for sure that Mr. Morgan himself had anything to do with it—he must've been a kid then, right?"

"*I* was a kid!" Maxwell yells. "That didn't stop the Morgans!"

Next to me, Leo steps closer to my side. I gulp.

"What are you going to do?" I ask. What I really mean is *What are you going to make me do?*

"The Morgans ruined our futures, so I'm going to ruin Mr. Morgan's. I'll keep him from handing the keys over by any means necessary."

I straighten. "You are not hurting him. *I* am not hurting him."

"I can't stand by and let him sell this house, Barnaby. If it was up to me, he'd be run out of Sunnyside. He wouldn't make another dime destroying someone's dreams."

"I'm not disagreeing that what you've been through is awful, but we need to be careful," I warn. The idea of being the face of Maxwell's revenge makes my stomach churn. "Mr. Morgan isn't going to let go of his livelihood. If he finds out you're sneaking around and working against him, he might—"

"What else can he do to me? I'm dead!" Maxwell growls.

Leo and I exchange glances. Maxwell may be dead, but we're not. Mr. Morgan can use his money to make our lives miserable. I think of all the hours Mom spends consoling clients whose partners drag their names and finances through the mud.

"There must be another way to finish your unfinished business," I say. "You just have to be smart about finding it. And the first step is making sure this house stays standing. Then you'll have more chances to connect with renters who can help you."

"There's no guarantee of that. And I've already told you: if this house sells, I'm coming with you."

Maxwell steps away, and it's like there's a canyon between us. Things had slowly been getting better between him and me, but any progress we made has been ruined. It feels like we're back to being on opposite sides, and suddenly, that's not quite what I want.

"I've got my plan. You've got yours," Maxwell says. "I'll be free of this place either way."

Then he disappears, leaving Leo and me alone.

"I don't like this," Leo says, a tremor in his voice. "We said we'd help him, but I'm with you—this sounds risky."

I place my hand on my brother's shoulder. "Then we need to get to work on our plan B of saving this house. Because if we don't, we may be in real trouble."

25

Maxwell doesn't reappear right away, even with Leo and me calling his name. He may have escaped into his own 1980s version of the world, but his frustration lingers in the attic. The air stays heavy, like after a thunderstorm. Eventually, Leo heads downstairs to read in the hammock, but I stick around.

Even if Maxwell is right about revenge being his unfinished business, I can't have my little brother or me getting caught in any cross fire with Mr. Morgan. I need to get him to focus on a safer bet: saving the house so he—and we—can live to fight another day.

But I can't convince him of anything if he doesn't talk to me.

I set up my tablet on the corner of my bed. Playing *Warricane* now might mess with Mom's internet connection speed, but it's worth the risk. This is an emergency.

The game takes a few minutes to start up, but the second its intro sound blares into the room, I scramble to turn it down so Mom doesn't hear. But it's enough to get Maxwell's attention.

The skin on the back of my neck prickles. He's in the room somewhere, watching me. He's not ready to talk yet, though. I can wait.

I log in with my username, BarnabusRex, and choose an easy quest: steal a rover from an alien base. Morris, Cru, and I compete on how fast we can complete this quest, and so far, I'm winning with under twelve minutes. But today, victory isn't going to be a stolen rover. It's going to be getting Maxwell to talk to me.

The game begins, and I send my character sneaking through the course, picking up potions and laser gun cartridges.

Five minutes in, Maxwell speaks. "Why do you skip those blue cubes?"

He points a semi-translucent finger at my tablet screen.

"Those are low-grade shields. I can only hold so much inventory, and I don't waste supply slots on anything that won't pack a huge punch."

"The red one you grabbed—that's higher grade?"

I nod. "It takes three blue cubes to equal one red. So I'd much rather have these."

"Ah."

We fall into silence, but he doesn't disappear.

A few minutes later, he says, "The stars in the background look so real. It's like you're actually in space."

"*Warricane* won a ton of awards for its graphics. There's an ice planet mission that almost makes me feel cold."

"I always wanted to go to space," he says.

I don't miss that he says that like it's in the past. He used to want something, but wanting is useless when you're stuck haunting a vacation rental. I think of the *E.T.* poster that hung in his room. I wonder what else he was interested in when he was alive and how many other dreams he let die when he woke up as a ghost.

I'm aware of his form nearby as I send my player into the dark alien base. I enter a room full of storage lockers to find a key. I pause the game.

I glance sideways at Maxwell. "You want to try?"

His eyes widen, our earlier tension forgotten. "Seriously? Can I?"

"Well, I'm guessing that if you can open a bag of chips, you should be able to put enough pressure on the screen to tap it. So there." I point to the image of a green locker. "Try opening that. One tap."

Maxwell trains his attention on the tablet. He shakes out his limbs, as if he's warming up for a race. Then he tentatively pushes a finger against the screen. Nothing happens. His face falls.

"Wait, hold on," I say. Maybe the pressure isn't enough.

He doesn't have any body warmth because he has no body. The touch sensors may not be picking him up. I run over to my suitcase and pluck out a stylus, then set it next to my tablet. "Pick that up and use it like a pencil to tap the screen."

Maxwell gives me a weak smile and concentrates. Slowly and shakily, the stylus rises in his ghost hand. His jaw tightens, and I can practically see the muscles in his arms tense as he pushes the stylus against the screen.

The green locker opens. A coin rises from it with a twinkling sound.

"Yes!" he screams. The stylus clatters to the floor. "I did it!"

His joy is contagious. I put out a hand for a high five. He obliges, and when his hand goes straight through mine, he simply laughs.

"This is amazing," he says, breathless, though I'm not even sure he breathes. "Can I—can I keep playing?"

"Sure." I give him a very basic tutorial, and I don't think I've ever seen him so happy. It's easy to forget that he's a ghost with a mission. Right now, he just seems like a regular kid getting to play the summer's hottest video game for the first time.

He's able to play for about ten minutes before his movements get sluggish. A line forms between his brows, and his arm starts to droop.

"What's wrong?" I ask.

"This takes up a lot of energy. You can have your game back." He sets down the stylus with a look of longing.

"You can play later, when you're at full strength again."

"Thanks." Then he pauses and his eyes narrow. "What's the catch?"

"What do you mean?"

"You're suddenly being nice. There has to be a reason."

"I'm always nice!"

Maxwell snorts, and to be honest, I don't defend myself. I admit I've been a bit aggressive in my attempts to get rid of him.

"I just want you to rethink this revenge plan," I say. "Mr. Morgan won't know that it's you—and not Leo and me—trying to take him down. I don't want you putting me or my family in danger when there could be another way out."

His face goes serious. "I don't want to put you guys in danger either, but we don't *know* if there's another way out. Getting back at Mr. Morgan has to be my unfinished business. It's the only thing that makes sense, the only thing I haven't tried."

I shake my head. "That can't be true. There are a lot of things that might count as unfinished business; you just need time to figure them out."

"I don't have time, Barnaby. You're leaving. This place will be a cookie bakery! I'm not going to throw away my chance at freedom."

My shoulders droop.

His voice is quiet when he speaks next. "How would you feel if this all happened to you? If someone tried to hurt the people you love and ended up killing you and separating you forever?"

I don't answer, but I feel everything he's trying to impart.

"I'm not going to change your mind, am I?" I ask.

"No," he says. "But I'll try to make sure nothing blows back on you and Leo, okay?"

His tone is determined and sincere in a way that makes me believe him. We're at a standstill, and there's nothing either of us can do to convince the other. All I can do is hope that I solve Maxwell's unfinished business before he tries to exact his revenge.

I sigh. "Okay. But I'm only agreeing to this because I *know* I'll beat you to a solution."

He catches the competitive ribbing in my voice. A smile spreads across his face. "Oh yeah? You think you're so smart, but I bet you didn't even notice that purple cube tucked behind the heat lamp," he says, gesturing to my screen.

Sure enough, a purple cube—the highest-level shield in

the game—peeks out from behind a part of the room that I'd always zoomed by. "What— How did you . . . ?"

He smirks. "I've got the brains and you've got the brawn, or at least the basic requirements for a human being to operate the game. Come on, let's try something harder."

"I haven't beat the expert-level Mountain Altar quest yet. Want to try that?"

"Okay. I bet I'll spot a dozen things you've missed."

I roll my eyes before I exit to the main menu. He settles into a spot next to me. When the Mountain Altar quest loads, he glances at me, excitement in his eyes.

I smile back. "Game on, ghost."

26

An hour later, I escape the attic for the fresh air of the patio. Leo is still lounging in the hammock with a graphic novel. The engineering team left after lunch, taking that life-altering yellow box with them. This would be a great time to melt away the tension in the hot tub, but no way I'm risking that again.

Mom relaxes outside, an icy glass in hand. A pitcher of iced tea, a couple of empty glasses, and a creased copy of the latest *Sunnyside Gazette* sit in the middle of table. Pao sprawls in the shade under her chair.

"All done with work?" I ask. My gaming earlier thankfully didn't draw her out of her office to complain about the network speed. I don't quite understand the idea of going on vacation just to spend half of it working, but then again, I don't understand a lot of what drives my parents.

"Yes. Everyone took the afternoon off to get an early start on July Fourth celebrations. Got any plans for the holiday tomorrow?" Mom asks.

I sit next to her, and she moves to pour me a glass. "Not really."

"No hanging out with friends here?"

I shake my head. "Don't have any." Saying it aloud stings, but it shouldn't. I'm the one who didn't even want to be here. When we arrived, all I wanted was to be at home, gaming with Cru and Morris, sleeping in my own bed. But now I actually feel lonely.

Mom frowns, as if remembering how much of a fight I put up weeks ago too. "I'm sorry, Barnaby. I know this isn't what you'd hoped for your summer, but Grandpa needs our help."

"I know."

When they first mentioned this extended trip, I'd asked why we didn't just hire movers to toss things in boxes over a long weekend and come home. Dad said the whole three weeks were necessary because Grandpa would need plenty of time letting go. We'd argued over it then, but I understand now. One year or four decades: grief over a loss doesn't have a set end date, if any.

Mom wipes away her frown, and when she speaks, she's cheerful. "Hey, I have an idea. Since it's a holiday, you deserve a break too. How about you see if your friends back home are up for some *Warricane*?"

I perk up. "I— That'd be great. Thanks, Mom."

She returns my smile. "Just for the holiday, though. Since I'm not planning to work at all, I won't need that internet juice."

I raise an eyebrow. I'm pretty sure *internet juice* isn't a real phrase, but I see what she's getting at. Our devices won't have to gladiator-battle over limited bandwidth.

"Then it's back to packing mode on Saturday, now that it's safe for all of us to enter Grandpa's house," Mom continues. "I wonder what they do in this town to celebrate Independence Day."

I recall the conversation with the pharmacist and her dog at the park. "I've heard there's a parade that goes down Main Street. The details are probably in the *Gazette*. You might want to get there early, though," I say before taking a sip of the iced tea.

"That sounds fun! I saw a picnic basket that I'm pretty sure is decoration, but it looks usable. We can pick up some bread and cheese at Fern's. I'll bring Leo to stake out a spot, and you and Dad can join us after your game."

A couple of weeks ago, I would've argued that last bit. I would've insisted I stay here and continue to play. But to be honest, it's been a while since I've done the whole patriotic-parade experience. Mom looks so tickled by the idea of a small-town parade; I don't want to fight her and take away that little glimmer of joy. "Sure."

Mom refills my glass with the last of the iced tea. Then she heads inside to mix another jug. I pull out my cell phone to type out an invitation to Cru and Morris on our group text thread, which has been woefully quiet the last few days. The ocean breeze picks up, and I close my eyes, letting the sun warm my face. It's so peaceful out here. I can see why Ms. Anita loathes the idea of a popular cookie bakery, with its long lines and busy kitchen, opening mere feet away from her window.

The rustle of paper snatches my attention, and I open my eyes just in time to see the *Sunnyside Gazette* lift off the table in the wind. I grab it right out of the air, and my gaze snags on bold text in the middle of the page.

Notice of Public Hearing: Sunnyside City Council will conduct a public hearing on the proposed commercial project by Blue Spoon Betty's.

Below it, in tiny font, is the address of Warner Place and a dozen lines of legal stuff.

A public hearing for the store that's planned for this property? Mr. Morgan did say there were some details to work out. It looks like the city council still has to approve the zoning change to allow a store to be built where a family home is. If I can go to this hearing and convince the city council to reject the change, the deal will be off. Plus, doing everything by the book and in front of the whole town means less chance for Mr. Morgan to try something sneaky against us.

Mr. Morgan will be forced to keep this as a house, and Maxwell can stay! He can pester another renter into helping him finish his business, if my brother and I aren't able to do it in the week we have left.

The hearing is on Monday, which means I only have a few days to figure out how to even talk to a city council, let alone convince them of zoning stuff I don't quite understand. Still, this is a real, viable plan B that seems more legal and less devious than whatever Maxwell might come up with. I have the whole weekend to—

I stop myself. Mom is giving me all day to game with Cru and Morris tomorrow. I peer down at my phone, the text box empty, the cursor waiting for me to make a move. I can throw this newspaper in the recycling bin, text my friends, and tomorrow relish a glimpse of the summer that I'm supposed to be having. That's what I wanted from the beginning, isn't it?

But Maxwell's question from earlier sticks to me. How would I feel if everything that happened to Maxwell happened to me? And worse, what if I had decades to stew about it and no one to help me?

I may have felt lonely earlier, when Mom asked about my July 4 plans, but it's nothing in comparison to the intense loneliness Maxwell has felt for years. His constant anger and pestering when we first met, his testing out new powers that help him push the boundaries of his world (to my chagrin), his singular focus on freeing himself: this is all a result of that bone-deep loneliness.

I may not agree with everything he says and does—especially not the possession part—but I'm starting to understand it. And to be honest, I get the feeling that in another day, another world, he and I might've been friends. We might have watched *Ghostbusters* together and laughed at the same parts. He might have checked out Leo's stack of graphic novels and asked for a recommendation or two. He holds a lot of anger that he could channel into some *Warricane* wins with Cru, Morris, and me.

A furry brush at my leg makes me jump. Pao has moved from under Mom's chair to under mine. She's seemed more at ease here since our day at the dog park. Stubborn, solitary Pao was able to make a friend. Even my grandpa, devastated by the loss of Grandma Violet, keeps asking about Ms. Anita and is clearly willing to date again (which is gross and not at all what I want to focus on right now). But if they can open their hearts, despite who they are and what they've been through, I can try too.

I raise my phone. Instead of texting my friends, I take

a photo of the notice of public hearing.

Gaming will have to wait. Maxwell is going down a dark path that could lead to terrible, wide-reaching mistakes. Someone needs to pull him back.

Somehow, that someone is going to be me.

27

I sit on the carpeted floor of Grandpa's living room with my tablet open on my lap. The art and family photos on the walls have been taken down, rugs rolled up, the furniture moved to make way for boxes and plastic crates. It's hard to believe this bare room was where Grandma snuck me handfuls of candy and where I ran interference between the sharp coffee table corners and then-toddler Leo's head.

Leo strolls over, Pao at his heels. "Shouldn't we be leaving for the parade?" he asks.

"Mom said it'll only be a few more minutes. They're finishing Grandpa's online application for benefits. Hey, what's your login for the e-collection for the library back home?"

"Nice try, but I'm not telling you my password. Hand it here: I'll type it in."

I do, and my brother taps away at the screen.

"What is it you're looking for?" he asks.

"Anything about how to speak at a public hearing. And maybe about the difference between commercial and residential zoning?"

Leo looks up from the tablet. "What do all those words even mean?"

"I don't know!" I groan and lower my head. Pao plops down next to me as moral support. "But we need to figure out how to convince the city council not to allow Warner Place to be demolished," I continue. "I don't know how their public hearings work—can we just show up? Do we have to RSVP like it's a birthday party or something?"

There's a crinkle of paper somewhere above me. Leo has picked up the notice that I'd clipped out from the newspaper and placed it beside me. "It doesn't say anything about RSVP'ing, so I bet we can just show up. And who's going to say no to a couple of kids interested in how government works?"

I raise my eyes to look at him. He's giving his most innocent, wide-eyed face. "Look at you, weaponizing your cuteness for the side of good."

"If you've got it, flaunt it." He hands me back my tablet. "Too bad we couldn't scope out a council meeting before the one on Monday."

"You know, they might live stream or record them," I say, my fingers already opening up a search bar. I look for any recent videos of Sunnyside city council meetings, and I almost cheer when a dozen results pop up. "There!"

I angle the tablet to Leo. He makes a face like he's smelled something rotten. "Some of these videos are two hours long! Are we seriously going to watch these right now? The parade..."

"Don't worry, I'll bookmark them for later. We can fast-forward through a couple tonight."

This small success raises my confidence. I open the library app again. "All right. Let's find something about zoning."

"You do that. I'm going to see what's taking them so long. Maybe grab a cookie out of Grandpa's secret stash."

Leo shuffles away into the kitchen, Pao trotting behind him at the mention of *cookie*. I stay seated, scrolling through result after result.

I don't know how much time has gone by until Leo reappears.

"Um, are you okay?" he asks.

I crane my neck up to look at him. "Huh? Why?"

"Your face—it was all scrunched up and confused."

I sigh. "That's because I *am* confused. I think I get the gist of what Mr. Morgan and Blue Spoon Betty's have to do. Everything on that block is homes, right? That means that area is designated residential. In order to build a store like Blue Spoon Betty's, they have to get this zone changed from residential homes to money-making commercial stuff or they have to request a variance, which is basically asking for special permission."

"And the city council—they're the ones that will give that permission?" Leo asks.

"I . . . I think so. Ugh. My brain hurts. I should've asked you to bring me some cookies." I set my tablet down.

The room comes flooding back to me then, and so does a sudden, unwelcome pang of sadness. Our family made so many memories here. Someone else is going to move in in a couple of weeks, and they'll decorate and make it their own. It'll be like Grandma and Grandpa were never here at all. I imagine it's hard for Grandpa to leave this life behind—not that he could control a lot of what led to his moving in with us. I wonder if it's worse for Maxwell, watching people erase the traces of him and his family in real time.

From the hallway to the bedrooms, a door slams, and the whole house shakes.

"Barnaby, Leo, we're done!" Mom calls.

I push up to standing. Every step I take toward the front door is one I've taken before in our visits past, but the motions feel different this time. They feel hollow.

My hand brushes the wall as I head out, and a rough patch grabs my attention. I glance down to find the imperfectly fixed hole I'd made in the wall years ago, when I'd knocked over a chair while chasing Leo. Grandma had shrieked at the sight of the damage. The sound scared Leo and made him cry. Later that afternoon, in the garage, Grandpa made me hold the flashlight as he rummaged around a creaky metal cabinet for patching supplies.

I run my fingers over the uneven plaster, a lump growing in my throat. I was wrong. This patch is lasting proof Grandma and Grandpa were here after all. The new owners might sand this down, paint over it, or throw a piece of furniture in front. But it'll stay part of this house, an almost-invisible but well-earned scar from when we made memories here. Like Maxwell's name by his attic window.

Leo steps to the side, to let me by. "Even if we're able to save Warner Place, Mr. Morgan needs to put in some serious work. It's so old. Everything makes a noise. The floorboards, the shower. Even the patio light makes a weird buzzy sound."

I pause. "You're right. It *is* old. And so is Ms. Anita's house."

I rerun the conversations I've had with her, each exchange replaying like a movie in my head. "She said that her house has some special protections because it was on some historic register. If we can do that with Warner Place, then they can't demolish it and put a bakery there!"

"That's a great idea," Leo says. "How do we do that?"

My excitement dips. "I have no idea. I guess I could do more research." My neck already hurts thinking about craning over the tablet for another few hours, searching for info on historic homes. "The council meets on Monday. How in the world am I going to fit in this much research? It feels like writing a huge book report that I just found out was due tomorrow."

"I know you won't like this idea, but I think it's our best bet," my brother says slowly.

I'm instantly wary. "What is it?"

"We should ask Mom for help."

I cringe. "No. She'll wonder why I'm asking! I can't exactly tell her it's to save our vacation rental so a ghost doesn't follow us home."

"Leave the ghost part out, then?"

"Do you have another excuse we can use? Because it's not like all kids run around saving historic homes during their summer vacations."

"Hmm . . . you're right. Not *all* kids."

I swear I see the lightbulb pop up over his head at the same time I have the idea. "You!" I blurt out. "Leo, you can ask her! If I ask, she'll be on alert. But she has no reason to worry you're up to something. She'll answer your questions, I'm sure of it."

Leo smiles. "Happy to weaponize my cuteness for the side of good."

28

By the time we arrive on Main Street, it's lined with lawn chairs and food coolers doubling as seats. The walk didn't take us long, but already Pao is panting, tired. I bend over to scoop her up.

Dad whistles, his arms full of beach chairs borrowed from the vacation house. "Whew, I wonder what time people started staking out their spots."

"The lady from the dog park did say we needed to get here before ten," I say. I pull the brim of my ball cap down to block out the harsh summer rays.

Mom shields her own eyes with her hand. "Where in the world are we going to sit?"

"Leave this to me," Grandpa says with a wink. He ambles over to an older white couple with matching Hawaiian shirts. After a minute, he waves us over.

Mom leads the way. The picnic basket from the house is weighed down with so many drinks and snacks that she leans slightly to the side as she walks. The couple Grandpa was talking to scoots their own beach chairs to the side, carving out a small space on the sidewalk for us.

"This is Amos and Billie," Grandpa says, clapping his hand on Amos's shoulder. "We were in the same ballroom dancing class."

Billie smiles, her bright red lipstick matching the American flags around us. "Your grandfather is quite the dancer. My Amos is so clumsy that we joke he actually has three left feet."

"Nothing wrong with dancing to the beat of your own drum!" Amos says, and the three of them laugh like it's something they've joked about for years. Amos moves his chair over a few more inches. "There, you should have enough room. Albert, if I'd known you were coming and bringing the family, we would've saved more space!"

"Just start dancing, honey. People will make room for us real quick," Billie says.

She brays out a laugh and slaps her knee. Amos sticks his tongue out at her, and it's easy to see how they've gotten along all these years. It was the same kind of loving silliness with Grandpa and Grandma.

Mom and Dad thank them and start setting up the

chairs. Leo, Pao, and I wait in the shade of the storefront behind us. It's a beach clothing store, selling lots of flowy dresses, big straw hats, and even the Hawaiian shirts that Amos and Billie are wearing. Assorted stuffed animals in the corner remind me of Ms. Anita, her daughter, and that self-bleating lamb stuffie. I wonder how Ms. Anita is spending the holiday.

"Remember: you can't just launch into the questions out of nowhere," I coach Leo. "Mom would totally see right through that."

Parade noise shields our conversation. In the distance, a pair of college kids set up a sound system by a flag-decorated podium. There's a squeak of speakers, a "Hello? Testing, one, two, three," then some indecipherable grumbling.

Leo snickers. "I know. You think this is the first time I've had to sneak an answer?"

I nod in respect. He's clever.

"I'm a little worried about how good you are at this. It makes me wonder how you've used your superpowers on me in the past," I joke.

Leo doesn't share my laughter. That only makes me wonder even more.

Before I can ask, he steps away from the storefront, smooths down his hair with his palms, then mutters, "Showtime."

He drifts over to where our parents have set up two chairs and laid a fluffy beach towel directly on the sidewalk cement. Dad and Grandpa are talking to Amos and Billie. Mom fishes a couple of juice boxes out of the picnic basket.

More paradegoers begin to arrive, scanning the sidewalks for any open space. I don't want to get cut off from our prime viewing area. Pao and I head back to the family too.

"Well, if you really like the style of that room, we can pick up some beach decorations on our way home," Mom says in response to whatever Leo's opening line was.

He smiles, and I can tell from the wide eyes that he's engaging maximum cuteness. "Wow, that'd be great! I wish they had more houses like our vacation one, though. Not all boxy and boring."

Mom chuckles. "I didn't know you were so into architecture."

"Watched a YouTube video on it," he says, the sweetness never leaving his voice.

I roll my eyes. What nine-year-old is casually on residential architecture YouTube? I keep my snark to myself, though, because whatever angle he's taking with Mom, it's working.

She hands him a juice box, and he dutifully takes a sip.

"I wish they weren't tearing it down," he says. He even adds a downward glance and a wistful sigh.

"Same. It's a gorgeous house."

"You think it's historic? Maybe we can get it on that register and they won't turn it into a bakery."

Mom pauses in thought.

I hold my breath. He really approached it head-on like that. If I'd posed that question so directly, Mom would've instantly suspected I was up to something (which I am, but that's not the point). But with curious, adorable Leo, she's quick to engage with his every question.

"It might have some historic value. But I doubt Mr. Morgan would want us interfering."

At the mention of Mr. Morgan, Amos snorts. "Humph. The Morgans. They've been here for generations, but you'd think they hate this place with as much as they're trying to ruin it."

Next to him, Billie's red lips press into a flat line, and even Grandpa's cheeriness drops a degree.

I raise an eyebrow. Everyone here seems to really dislike the Morgans. And after what the Morgans did to Maxwell and his family, I don't feel bad about working against them and Blue Spoon Betty's.

I move closer. "How would we get something on the historic register?" I ask.

This time, when Mom pauses, it's because she's trying to figure out why I'm suddenly interested too.

So I add, "Just curious. Leo watched that video on my tablet."

Mom can't get mad at brothers bonding by sharing electronics. "Ah, well, different places have different rules and processes. But usually a property has to meet some requirements for age, historical significance, whether it looks pretty close to the way it was originally built, stuff like that. Then you submit an application for that historic designation to whoever makes the decision."

"That's the planning commission here," Billie cuts in. "Then they recommend the city council approve the designation or not. Our neighbor tried to get her house designated as historic, but it turns out she'd totally faked that John Steinbeck stayed there. It was such a scandal!"

"Mr. Morgan said they did some renovation of the house, but it's pretty close to the way it was originally built—that vintage beach charm," I say. "So we'd just have to find some reason the house is historically significant?"

I realize I've overstepped when Mom frowns. "Barnaby, this can be a long, complicated process. Why the sudden interest in the vacation house?"

"We just really like the house! That hammock? That huge TV? You and Dad made such a good choice," Leo cuts in. He even hugs her. Whatever suspicion was in her eyes dies down. The kid has skills.

"I'm glad. Yes, you'd need some solid evidence that the house has historic value. Maybe even get some local historians or organizations to write letters of support. But, kids, we're only here for another week. That's not nearly enough time to start the process."

With the city council meeting on Monday, it might be enough to throw a wrench into Mr. Morgan's zoning request.

"And if you've only got a week, I wouldn't spend it riling up the Morgans. They may seem nice, but they're sharks," Amos adds. "Totally shut me out after I hurt my leg on their faulty equipment."

He raises his left leg as if it pains him. Amos was hurt on the job? Was he the one whose injury inspired Maxwell's dad to get all the workers together?

"The union," I whisper.

Only Leo hears me. He sends me a questioning look. I don't have time to explain.

"The Warners," I say more loudly. "The vacation house we're staying at: it used to be theirs. Do you know what happened to the family?"

Amos's face falls. "The same thing that happens to anyone who crosses the Morgans."

Those speakers in the distance squeak again. "Welcome to the annual Fourth of July parade!" someone announces in a very practiced, overly chipper voice.

Cheers erupt around us.

It's so at odds with the chill running down my spine from what Amos said. The parade is about to start, and there's little time before the marching band drowns out all other noise.

I sidle closer to Amos. "Do you think the Morgans did something bad to the Warners?"

He shakes his head. "Don't you worry about them, kid. Your grandpa told me about the hot tub, but it sounds like they weren't too mad. I'll tell you this, though: if you ever hear anything bad about the Morgans, believe it."

"Parade time," Grandpa cuts in, oblivious to what Amos and I had been talking about. He picks up Pao and sets her in his lap as he sits in a beach chair. "There! Can you see?" he asks, as if expecting the dog to respond.

When I turn back to Amos, he's already chatting with Billie, and I don't want to drag him down with more conversation. He confirmed what we suspected about the Morgans: that's all I need.

I look for a place to sit. Dad positions himself on the edge of the beach towel, with Leo next to him. Mom sets down the basket, and before she sits, something inspires me to hug her. I do, and she actually freezes in surprise.

"Everything okay, sweetie?" she asks.

I let go. My cheeks go red. I don't know what came over me. "Yeah, I just . . . I'm sorry I gave you a hard time about coming here."

She smiles. "It's all right. I know you had a different idea of how you wanted your summer to go. Are you having a good time, though?"

"I wouldn't necessarily say I'm having a good time." I think of Maxwell welcoming us by ripping open the bag of chips and trying to kick me out of the attic. But then I think of ice cream with Grandpa, discovering my little brother's sneaky talents, and gaming with Maxwell. "But it hasn't been terrible. And who doesn't love a parade?"

She chuckles. "Good enough. I'll take it."

The speaker booms again with someone reciting logistical information about where people can sit and stand, being conscious of our neighbors, picking up our trash, and so forth. Mom takes the remaining chair, and I plop down on the beach towel too.

I lean close to my brother. "Good job. I think we're one step closer to getting Maxwell off our backs."

Leo smiles for a moment before he turns to the parade route and sighs. "Do you think he likes parades?"

We both stare out at Main Street, empty of cars but lined with people waving miniature American flags, slathered in sunscreen, soaking in the increasing warmth of the sun. "If Maxwell likes parades, it's probably been ages since he's seen one."

I pull out my phone and prop it in front of us.

"What are you doing?" Leo asks.

"Recording some of it for him."

I grab a full juice box and try to finagle it so the cell phone stays still, its camera trained on the parade route.

Out of the corner of my eye, I notice my brother continuing to stare at me, silently. Then the sound of a marching band strikes up a couple of blocks away, and he turns to squint in that direction.

I think he might've been smiling. But whether at me or at the band, I don't know. It must be the band, I decide. Who doesn't love a parade?

29

My arms are jelly after an entire weekend of packing at Grandpa's. It turns out that "But I'm only twelve!" does not save me from having to move huge boxes of very heavy, very delicate china or from holding the massive bed frame still while Dad unscrews the headboard.

Jelly arms or not, I have a council meeting to attend.

Ignoring the ache in my biceps, I focus on buttoning the one collared shirt I brought to Sunnyside. It's not that fancy—it's light blue, dotted with tiny palm trees wearing sunglasses—but I want to make a good impression. This is the first and last chance I'll get to convince the city council to prevent the demolition of this house.

A knock on the stairwell distracts me from the buttons.

Leo strolls in a moment after. "Okay, alibi set. Mom and Dad think you're taking me to the library for a graphic novel talk."

"Great, I—" My voice withers when I take in what Leo's wearing. "Seriously? You *have* to wear the same palm tree shirt that I do?"

"What? It's the only thing I brought that has a collar!"

"Ugh, me too! We're going to look so weird if we walk in all matchy-matchy."

Maxwell materializes between the mirror and me and laughs. "This is amazing. No backing out now."

Leo and I had briefed Maxwell about the historic registry after the parade. In the few hours we'd spent here instead of at Grandpa's, we researched the house's history. We looked for every reason why Mr. Morgan couldn't hand over this house to someone with a wrecking ball.

I sigh. "I know, I just wish I had something less cringeworthy to wear. I'm already nervous about this whole thing."

"Why?" Maxwell asks. "We have a good reason to declare this historic: its significance in the labor movement in Sunnyside! Our living room is where the construction bigwigs tried to strongarm my dad. Our kitchen is where my dad and his crew met late at night to talk union strategy over coffee and Mom's key lime pie."

Maxwell's excitement is contagious, but it's not enough to blow through the thick fog of anxiety. "I know, but if they deny the historic designation and don't buy our reasons for rejecting Mr. Morgan's zoning request, then this place will be rubble in a few weeks and you'll be making a nice, cozy home in *me*."

"Then all the more incentive to succeed, don't you think?"

I groan and finish buttoning my shirt.

"Council meeting starts in fifteen minutes," Leo says. "We should go."

Maxwell drifts to the window. He runs his fingers along the carving of his name on the wall and heaves a sigh. "Good luck. You'll let me know how it goes?"

My heart squeezes at the sadness in his voice. I thought I was anxious, but Maxwell has so much more riding on this meeting than I do. "Actually, um, if you want to come, I might have an idea of how you can hitch a ride."

He turns to look at me.

"Not with me!" I say, backing away. "Ms. Anita had mentioned her daughter accidentally bought a lamb doll she thought was possessed. Have you tried inhabiting someone or something other than me?"

Maxwell taps his chin. "I was surprised I was even able to possess you—I didn't test it out with anyone else, and you did make me promise not to. Maybe your dog—"

"Nothing *ever* happens to the dog!" I growl.

He splays his hands out to placate me. "Okay, okay, it was just a thought. But then how will I get to the hearing? Unless you want to lend me a toe or something."

Leo jumps in. "Try this!" He holds out the astronaut action figure Grandpa bought him.

Maxwell's eyes widen. "I've been getting stronger. This might just work."

"It's worth a shot," I say. "If your ghost powers can extend to city hall, you can listen in and give us hints on what to do."

"All right, here goes," Maxwell says. He stands up straight and shuts his eyes tight. Then he disappears from view. Suddenly, the astronaut waves the American flag in its hand.

"Did—did I do it?" a voice comes from the astronaut.

Leo gives the action figure a tiny high five. "You sure did! How is it? You think you'll be able to make it to city hall?"

Astronaut Maxwell gives a jerky nod. "It feels more draining to inhabit an object, but I should have enough energy to hold on for a while." His arms move in an equally jerky motion. "This is amazing. I could get used to this!"

"Well, hopefully you won't have to. If everything goes well at city hall, you'll get your chance to free yourself altogether." With one last pat of my hair and outfit check in the mirror, Leo, Maxwell, and I head downstairs.

The city council room is all stately dark wood and large windows. Leo walks ahead on the faded teal carpet and seats himself in the first row of chairs facing the council. He perches Astronaut Maxwell on the chair next to him, and I sit too.

At the front of the room loom five black leather chairs. Four are occupied by men with various degrees of facial hair ranging from a neat goatee to a Santa-level beard. The other chair holds a familiar, feminine face.

"Serenity!" I call out.

Serenity from the dog park brightens when she sees me. She's in a pink blouse and tan pants, a touch more formal than her dog-walking gear.

"Barnaby! You're spending your summer vacation at a council meeting? Kids these days," she teases.

The city clerk, a young Black man with a flat-top haircut and red bow tie, clears his throat. "Can everyone take their seats, please?" he says.

At his request, a dozen people filter into the rows of chairs near us.

The council member in the middle is in a white polo shirt, his hairy arms red from the sun. I wonder if he was out all day for the Fourth of July parade too. I doubt his mom chased him down to wear sunscreen like ours did. A bronze nameplate in front of him reads *Jim Carn, Council President*.

"All right, first order of business," Jim announces, "I hope everyone had a pleasant holiday weekend. I heard

Henry almost burned down his house with his grill antics again."

The councilman to the right of him, Henry, turns red. Well, a brighter red. He already looked sunburned, his nose and brow a painful pink. The rest of the council begins to rib Henry, and the sound of chatter throughout the council room rises.

This seems a friendly enough group. I angle in my chair to check out the other attendees. Four elderly women with matching green *Dames for Driftwood* T-shirts are spread across the back row. I didn't realize driftwood needed so many advocates. Across the aisle, a bald Latino man clutches a clipboard packed with papers full of signatures. Next to him, a little girl younger than Leo is slumped far down in her seat, making no effort to disguise how bored she is.

Then the doors boom open and in marches Mr. Morgan. I gulp. He is the only one in a full business suit and likely the one person in Sunnyside who owns a leather briefcase. He lowers his designer sunglasses just enough to eye the room. His eyes narrow when they land on me.

"What are you doing here?" he asks. It sounds friendly on the surface, but I catch the hint of a threat in it.

I gulp. "It's—it's a public hearing. That means I can be here."

He snorts derisively. "I know what *public* means, kid."

"What a sleazeball," Astronaut Maxwell says next to me. "Launch me at him. I'll plant this flag in his ear."

I suppress a smile and straighten in my seat. The clunky, vinyl-covered chair is uncomfortable, but I don't think that's the reason I'm so unsettled. It's hard enough psyching myself up to talk to the city council. I figured Mr. Morgan would be here, but seeing him make a late, dramatic entrance—and zeroing in on me—adds a whole other layer of intimidation.

At the front of the room, Jim speaks. "Okay, first official item on the agenda is the variance request for Warner Place. Dean, take it away!"

The city clerk reads out some details about the property request that I can't keep up with. But the city council listens intently. One of them moves aside his bronze nameplate reading *George Lee* to make room for a yellow notepad. He scribbles down some notes.

"And what was the planning commission's recommendation?" Jim asks once the city clerk is finished.

Dean squints to read something off his laptop screen. "They recommend you approve the variance request."

"Wait, is that it?" I call out, alarmed. "Don't I get to speak?"

Dean glances up from his laptop. "Don't worry. The public comment period is next. You'll have to fill out a speaker slip to get in line to speak."

"A what?"

Leo places his hand on my arm. "I gotcha. I filled one out already."

Dean grabs a small stack of cards from the corner of his desk. "First commenter is Barnaby Vargas. Please approach the podium."

My breath whooshes out of me. My head is still reeling from the twists and turns of the last few minutes. And now I'm up first?

I start to panic. I'm not prepared for this. A ghost stuck on this earth for decades has his entire existence in my hands. *I* have my entire existence in my hands. If I'm not able to save Warner Place, that ghost will take over my body instead.

I make the mistake of meeting Mr. Morgan's glare. His face is an icy calm, but there's an anger in his eyes that I recognize from the café, when he demanded Eleanor redo his coffee order. He can't stand to have something not go his way, and here I am, rising up to challenge him.

Suddenly, everything feels like too much of a weight to carry. My jelly arms can't possibly support this.

Both Leo and Maxwell notice my hesitation.

Leo sends me a questioning look. "Are you okay? You're sweating . . . a lot."

"You can do this, Barnaby," Maxwell says. "I need you to. Please."

The *please* is what gets me. He's not forcing me, even though he could. Instead, he's pleading for my help. He's asking me, as a friend.

I stagger to my feet and try to move my legs.

I can't.

And it's not Maxwell's doing. I, plain and simple, am frozen with fear.

"Don't worry," Maxwell's voice echoes in my head. "I've got this."

The astronaut action figure suddenly keels over. Then with a head-to-toe tingle and a hair-raising surge of energy, my body begins to approach the podium.

30

Maxwell stops me right in front of the podium. I grip its sides hard. I'm holding myself up and steady, and so is Maxwell.

"You're seriously going to let that *kid* talk?" Mr. Morgan's voice booms from the back. It's laced with something menacing, and some of the council members flinch.

Then I remember what Amos told me at the parade: if you hear anything bad about the Morgans, believe it.

Dean, the city clerk, shushes him, though. At least not everyone's intimidated by that family.

When we'd first met, Mr. Morgan had pinned me as a lone wolf, just like him. I didn't think anything of it then, but I hate that he might have seen some real similarities between us—and I'm starting to see them too.

I haven't spotted Mr. Morgan around town with

anyone who looks like they could be his friend: only business associates and people he pays. But it's not like I went out of my way to get to know anyone in Sunnyside.

Mr. Morgan and I both pursue what we want at all costs. He's determined to make this big sale go through, even if it will ruin neighborhoods and lives—including ghost lives. And haven't I spent the last two weeks ruthlessly trying to get back to that ideal summer I'd hoped for?

My legs buckle, and I can't tell if it's my energy failing or Maxwell's.

"Are you okay?" Maxwell says only to me.

I gulp, unable to answer through the question screeching in my mind: Am I really on the path to becoming like Mr. Morgan?

I don't *ever* want to be like him.

I want to be like Leo, always ready with a kind word, a helping hand, and a jacket. Like Pao, an old dog who learns new tricks. Like Grandpa, who lost so much but isn't letting that close off his heart forever. With every story about Grandma we tell, every family photograph we find, he works to heal, and he may even be ready to date. (Actually, I don't want to be so much like Grandpa in that last regard.)

All this time, I thought the only place I could be with friends is back at home. That's not true, though. There can be friends all around us, if only we look. That's what

Leo, Pao, and Grandpa seem have figured out: opening themselves up to friendship—wherever and in whatever form—means opening themselves up to joy.

And now I've figured that out too.

"I'll be fine," I whisper to Maxwell. "Thanks for helping me. Just stick with me a little longer, okay?" I don't want him suddenly fleeing my wobbly legs and leaving me a big nervous heap on the council room floor.

His response is automatic. "Of course."

The council members lean forward, waiting for me to speak. Serenity gives me an encouraging smile.

I clear my throat with a cough and, with shaky hands, reach for the phone in my pocket. Leo and I had typed out our notes so I wouldn't forget to mention anything.

"Hi, um, Your Honors," I begin.

A few chuckles erupt around the room, and I instantly feel my face go hot. Maxwell doesn't let me falter or flee.

"You don't have to call us that," Serenity says, her face kind. "But please, go on."

"Thanks. Um, I don't think you should approve the request. They want to make Warner Place a cookie bakery."

Somewhere, a derisive snort shoots out, clearly meant to be heard. I can tell exactly who it's from. Serenity sends a momentary glare in that direction.

"I know I'm only here for a little while, but even I see that Sunnyside is losing what makes it Sunnyside. My grandpa's lived here for years. So has our neighbor for the summer. And they talk about the Grand Seabird Hotel I'll never stay at, the boardwalk shops I'll never stroll through—"

"Bigger and better things are coming," Jim, the council president, interjects cheerily.

"But will bigger and better things leave space for the small, already-wonderful things? Like friendship bracelets and ice-cream shops and mom-and-pop restaurants."

Jim's face goes soft at the mention of friendship bracelets. He must be thinking of his granddaughter, the one Grandpa says is my age, and her small boardwalk side business.

Council member Henry sniffles too. "Ye Olde Hot Dog Kingdom really did have the best bratwurst."

George pats him on the back sympathetically.

Their emotional responses encourage me. "Warner Place has been around over a century. Getting rid of it would be like chipping away further at Sunnyside's soul."

Behind me, one of the Dames for Driftwood starts clapping. Another cups her hands around her mouth and yells a "You tell 'em, kid!"

One council member looks completely unswayed. In fact, he looks bored. I squint to read his name plate: Byron Bothers.

Byron twirls the pen in his hand. "Thank you for your

concern. But this proposal isn't going to ruin Sunnyside—it's going to revitalize it by bringing in more business."

Yanked out of their nostalgia, every council member except Serenity nods. It's then that I see a half inch of ribbon peeking out of Byron's shirt pocket, as if he'd stuffed it there haphazardly before the meeting. It's white, with blue anchors.

I reach for a tissue in my own pocket and pretend to blow my nose, just so I can cover up talking to Maxwell. "That ribbon in Byron's pocket—is that one of the Morgans'?"

"Yup, looks like it," Maxwell confirms. "That's not good. But there's hope for the others. Keep trying to convince them."

I lower the tissue. "Even so, there are more reasons to keep Warner Place. It has historical value. It belongs on the Sunnyside historic registry."

Murmuring breaks out, and this time, Byron sets down his pen. His eyes narrow with annoyance. "And what's the historic significance of the property?"

I break eye contact with him. It feels like I'm in trouble at the principal's office, which is not the most pleasant sensation. "It was, um, the unofficial headquarters of the union movement in Sunnyside," I say, reading the notes off my phone. "Back in the 1980s, construction workers regularly met there to—"

"Humph, there's no construction union in Sunnyside," Mr. Morgan interrupts. I whirl around. He is no longer lurking at the back of the room. He looms a few feet away now, as if about to bump me away from the podium.

The city clerk leaps to his feet. "Excuse me, it's not your turn to speak. You'll have to fill out a slip to address the council. It's protocol."

Mr. Morgan scoffs. "I should be allowed to defend my variance request against these lies."

I stumble over my own words. "Well, I mean, there isn't a union, but—"

"See?" His voice rises as he addresses the council and the entire room. "This kid has been trouble since his family arrived. Did you know he almost ruined his beloved, allegedly historic Warner Place by flooding the hot tub?"

"I didn't almost ruin it!" I counter. "You said—"

Mr. Morgan talks over me like I'm not even speaking. "He's lying about the hot tub—"

"You have to stop him!" Maxwell urges in me, kicking out a flare of energy.

"—and he's lying about the house being historic."

"Don't let him do this, Barnaby. Please!"

"This is absurd. There is no union in Sunnyside—"

My voice echoes through the room. "Because your family drove their leader out of town!"

The room goes silent. The rage on Mr. Morgan's face gives way to shock.

"What . . . what did you just say?" Mr. Morgan asks, pale.

At this, Dean positions himself between me and Mr. Morgan and shoves a pen and blank speaker slip in his direction. "Protocol. Let the kid speak."

"Yes. Barnaby here has two more full minutes. And one more word out of turn, Mr. Morgan, and the city clerk has full authority to bar you from the room," Serenity announces. "Isn't that right, Dean?"

Without taking his eyes off Mr. Morgan, Dean nods sharply with authority. "That's right, Councilwoman Ford."

Grimacing, Mr. Morgan snatches the pen and slip. My stomach flip-flops. I sure got everyone's undivided attention with that outburst.

"Keep going," Maxwell whispers in my head. "You only have a couple of minutes!"

"There is no union," I begin slowly, "because Mr. Morgan's family intimidated the Warners into leaving town. Gene Warner was trying to organize the people who worked for the Morgans. They wanted better health care and real breaks."

"I remember this!" one of the Dames shouts. "After Amos Henderson's leg was crushed!"

"Protocol!" Jim, the council president, snaps. "Fill out a slip!"

He's certainly on Mr. Morgan's side too. That's two out of the five council members I have no hope of winning over.

But I go on. "The Morgans gifted Gene some purposely tainted shortbread to stop him from showing up and voting in the union election. Unfortunately, Gene's son, Maxwell, was the one who ate it. It didn't just make him sick—it killed him. After he died, the Warners fled town."

The council room erupts in activity. Everyone in the room begins speaking at once. The council members debate with each other until their faces redden. The Dames trade teary-eyed memories about that dark moment in Sunnyside history. Dean spreads his arms out, blocking an irate Mr. Morgan from reaching me and the podium.

Then council member Henry shushes the room. "That's a serious accusation. Do you have any proof?"

"Of course not," Mr. Morgan cuts in. "Because it's not true!"

"Proof," I whisper to Maxwell. "Is there any proof?"

I feel his presence weaken for a moment, and his voice sounds suddenly faint. "No. There isn't. I—I ate it all, remember?"

I gulp and grab the tissue again to hide my chatter.

"The only way I know about the poison shortbread is through you."

"Can you tell them about me?"

"If I tell them I'm being possessed by the ghost of the murdered Warner boy, our cause is as good as lost. There's no way anyone's going to listen to me then." I blow my nose, and Mr. Morgan's gaze narrows, like he can sense I'm stalling. "Worse, what would they do to me, Maxwell? Would they take me away for psychiatric review or punish me for lying to the council?"

I strain to think of any way that revealing Maxwell's presence will convince the city council to save Warner Place.

I come up with nothing.

"Then don't," Maxwell says, his voice somber. He must have come to the same realization I did. "I—I can't do that to you. I said I wouldn't let this blow back on you or your family. Don't tell them about me, Barnaby. It's okay."

He's willing to risk his revenge—and being tethered to this world—for me. A lump grows in my throat.

I lower the tissue and gaze up at the council. Maxwell wants to keep me and my family safe, and that unfortunately means backing down. "All of the events line up. If you really look at the facts and the timing of what happened those days in December 1984, I think you'll agree something is fishy. But proof?" I let out a pained sigh. "No, I don't have any. It's—it's just a theory."

A few of the council members shake their heads, like I knew they would. Serenity, her brow furrowed, sighs. Dean politely informs me that my time to speak is up. I turn my back on the council, my chest tight.

Mr. Morgan, smug, takes his turn at the podium, only to say, "This whole discussion is ridiculous. I trust the council to do the right thing—the only thing that makes sense." The way he spits out *makes sense* is a punch to the gut, as if everything I said and everything about me is preposterous.

Then Jim, the council president, puts on his glasses. "It's time to vote." He calls for a show of hands. He and three council members vote to approve Mr. Morgan's request to let a business be built on Warner Place property. Only Serenity votes no.

Dean repeats the results, his voice solemn. "The variance request for commercial zoning is approved."

When Maxwell sobs, I'm the only one who can hear him.

31

I don't return to my seat. I plod straight down the aisle, toward the main doors. Leo scrambles to follow me, the astronaut action figure tucked under his arm.

The moment I exit the building, my legs suddenly go stiff.

"We can't leave yet. This can't be over," Maxwell begs. He pulls away slightly, the upper half of his body drifting next to me.

Leo frowns when he sees Maxwell. "We lost. I'm so sorry we couldn't convince them to save your home."

Maxwell's ghost flickers, as if the energy he's drawing from is fading—or surging. "I shouldn't have gotten my hopes up. I should've known this wouldn't work."

The words come out low and desperate, and a crack forms in my heart.

"It was worth a try, and we did our best," I say. "If

it had been a fair fight—if the council members weren't already on the Morgans' side—we would've won."

Maxwell's rattled stare doesn't steady. His image flickers faster. "We did our best with *your* plan, Barnaby. You thought you could buy me time to figure out my unfinished business. But I know what my unfinished business really is: it's revenge."

My arms begin to tingle; then I find myself being dragged back toward the city hall doors.

"No!" I tense my muscles and attempt to fight Maxwell's otherworldly control. I imagine my body going statue still, my feet sinking into quicksand. I barely manage to get my legs to stop. "What are you doing?"

"I can't let him get away with what his family did to me. He can't just hand over my house to those cookie people. We'll scare him into taking it all back, lock him in a room if we have to!"

Both Leo and I gasp.

"Maxwell, no!" Leo begs. He wraps his hands around my torso and locks his fingers together. The astronaut action figure clatters onto the boardwalk concrete. Leo is trying to keep my ghost-ridden body from going back inside too.

I try to reason with Maxwell. "You can't go after him. No one else knows about you. They're going to see *me* trying to hurt Mr. Morgan. They'll throw me in jail. You can't do this."

"But revenge is my unfinished business."

"You don't *know* that," Leo strains to say. He pulls hard at me, and his efforts are helping me stay grounded. "You said you didn't have any idea what your unfinished business was. That's why we tried to find your family, to see if they knew!"

"Decades. I've been here decades," Maxwell says. His voice is gravelly with emotion. "I've had over forty years to think about how to free myself. This is the only thing I haven't tried. My home is going to be destroyed. I can't stay there, in a soulless cookie bakery. I have nowhere to go."

Maxwell's power strengthens, and my right leg betrays me and takes a step forward.

Despair washes over me like a wave I didn't see coming. I'm submerged, struggling to breathe, grasping for anything to pull me out of the water. But then there's a life preserver: an approach I hadn't even considered.

The words I say next come out effortlessly, as if they were only waiting to be said.

"You do have somewhere to go, Maxwell," I say. "Come with us."

The internal push against my limbs stops. I almost topple back onto my brother.

"What did you say?" Maxwell asks, wary.

"I said come with us." The words are as easy to say the

second time. That's how I know I'm sure. "I don't know how long it'll take to finish your unfinished business, but we'll keep working on it together. You said you can't stay in the cookie bakery—"

"Which is weird, because honestly, that's a dream come true for me," Leo cuts in.

"I can't eat, remember?" Maxwell says, a hint of annoyance in his voice. But at least it's not all-out revenge-driven anguish.

"What I'm saying is that you need a home," I continue. "You won't have yours anymore. So come share ours. Stick with us a little longer."

Leo smooths down his shirt with his palms and frowns at me. "But, Barnaby, he can't leave Warner Place property without inhabiting another body. That means . . ."

"That means he's going to have to haunt me, I know," I say with a deep exhale. Acknowledging that doesn't scare me as much as I'd thought. I meet Maxwell's gaze. "You can be pushy and annoying, but you're not cutthroat like Mr. Morgan. We know now that you can at least switch out and spend some time in that astronaut action figure. And hey, who knows how your ghost powers are going to grow and change? Maybe in a few years we can find you a creepy puppet to move into. My friends Cru and Morris would actually get a kick out of that. They can help with the unfinished business too."

Maxwell is quiet at first. "No one has ever volunteered like this before."

I shrug. "Well, no one's accidentally triggered the evolution of your powers with a homemade Ouija board either. Or tried to banish you with pizza seasonings."

"I don't understand. You're going to let me haunt you? And come back with you to your home? Why would you do this?"

"I can't stop thinking about what you asked me: How would I feel if everything that happened to you happened to me? I'd be angry. But I'd also be sad: the kind of deep sad that makes me mean, that would make me do anything to stop it, even if it wasn't the best idea."

Maxwell's ghost form flickers again.

I continue. "And after decades of that, I'd still miss the same things: a cozy home, a family, and good friends. We—Leo and I—have that. So you can come live with us. You can be part of *us*."

My body begins to shake, as if the ground is quaking beneath me. But nothing else around us—the palm trees, the people laughing on the beach, the ice-cream cart with the red umbrella—moves. I gurgle in surprise. "What—what's happening?"

"I don't know!" Maxwell cries.

Something electric crackles in the air. Maxwell's image begins to lighten, and he's no longer a shadow or a half torso. A flash of light brightens the world around us, as if the sun trained its rays on us for a moment, and suddenly Maxwell is his full self, apart from me.

He stretches out his hands. He studies them, then his own legs. Maxwell is still translucent—I can see the trees swaying in the wind behind him. But now he's growing fainter.

"What are you doing?" I ask. "You can't leave my body without getting lassoed back to Warner Place."

"I'm not doing anything," he says, his voice careful. "I feel that pull, but it's not to Warner Place." His eyes meet mine, and his have grown wide, in awe. "I'm getting pulled up."

We both raise our gazes.

"They're there, in the stars. Mom and Dad," Maxwell whispers.

All I see are blue sky and seagulls. Then an eerie but familiar scent hits my nose: sugar and key limes.

"Your unfinished business . . ." Leo says. He inches closer to me. "He's moving on. Barnaby, I think maybe you finished Maxwell's unfinished business!"

"It wasn't revenge," I realize, my mind hurtling through everything that's happened in the past few weeks. "Family. Your unfinished business was reconnecting with family. But you couldn't do it because your parents were gone."

"And when you offered your family, it was . . . it was like the same thing." Maxwell sniffles and smiles at me. It's as bright as the flash of light earlier, but it's the kind of glitter that doesn't force my eyes shut. It's a warm glow that feels as welcoming as the morning sun.

My heart squeezes. I did it! I freed Maxwell.

His gaze shifts from joyful to anxious. "I—I have to go. They're calling me." He gulps, then puts on a tentative but hopeful smile. "I think I've been on Earth way past my curfew anyway."

I laugh, and there's a sadness in it that I hadn't expected. "Go on, get out of here."

Maxwell continues to fade. He drifts toward Leo and me. "Thank you. I'm sorry for all the trouble I caused, but I—I couldn't have done any of this without both of you."

I smile, and when Maxwell tries to pat me on the shoulder, his hand goes straight through me. Leo sniffles as Maxwell steps back, raises his gaze toward the sky, and disappears.

The wind picks up gently. It flits over the sand, ruffles our hair, soars through the palm leaves. The sun is pleasant on our skin, the air scented with sea salt and popcorn. Sunnyside really isn't all that bad of a place.

"You!" a voice behind us screeches.

Leo and I twist around to find Mr. Morgan stomping toward us.

"Pack your bags, boys. You're out of here."

32

The minivan shakes when Dad tosses his bag into the trunk. Mom slides her laptop bag much more gently into the front passenger seat, and I help Leo carry his duffel bag down the steps.

"He's not even offering another place to stay or shelling out for a cheap hotel," Dad gripes. "Did you see how expensive his car is? He can afford it."

Immediately after the council meeting, Mr. Morgan called my parents and said that there'd been "an egregious violation of the terms and conditions of our vacation-rental contract." Simply put, we had to vacate Warner Place as soon as possible. Whatever language Mr. Morgan and his lawyers had used, it was serious enough for Mom to bring her empty suitcase out of the closet.

Mom sighs. "Even if we fight it, it'll take days, weeks.

It's a good thing Grandpa's almost packed up anyway. We'll spend the night there and see what's left to do."

"We might get back home early, then. You'd like that, wouldn't you, guys?" Dad says to Leo and me.

A few weeks ago, the answer would've been an instant yes. But Sunnyside has grown on me. I can see why Grandpa wanted to stay after Grandma died. Still, it'll be nice to be back home, with my friends, my computer, and nothing to do during the day other than catch up my *Warricane* character level. I'm already planning on asking Cru and Morris if Leo can join our team.

"Mr. Morgan will like us skipping town early," Leo grumbles.

Mom sighs, but she's not upset. She and Dad, though frustrated at our forced early checkout, were proud of us for being, as Leo had spun it, "so civically engaged." They found out we were at the council meeting and so we told them everything. Well, almost everything. We left out the details about murders and ghosts, but Mom seems pleased to hear my brother and I bonded over research and public speaking. Dad said he was happy I'd done something other than mope around and complain for an afternoon, and I know there's some truth in that joke.

Mom picks up Pao and sets her in the van. "All right, I think that's everything. Boys, I'm going to do one last walk-through of the house to see if there's anything I missed. You want to join me?"

I peer up at Warner Place, shielding my eyes from the bright sun. The house may still be standing—for now—but it's no longer a home that needs saving. Maxwell is gone, off to wherever comes next for ghosts like him and his parents. "No. I got everything I need."

Mom and Dad disappear into the house, and the sound of the door opening nearby grabs our attention. Ms. Anita strolls out from next door, a platter of croissants in hand. "I'm sad to see you leave so soon. I thought you were here until the end of the week. I got you a little parting gift, though."

"Croissants!" Leo squeals. "Can I take an extra one for my parents to share? They're inside."

Of course he thinks of them.

"Take however many you can carry," Ms. Anita says with a smile. "You must have a long drive back home."

I eagerly grab a croissant and thank her. "Actually, we're squeezing into Grandpa's place for a night or two first. Might be a little cramped, but we'll manage."

She chuckles. "It's no Warner Place, that's for sure. They don't make houses like this anymore. Well, it was a pleasure being neighbors with you. Safe travels, Vargas family."

She's about to turn to reenter her home when an idea

strikes me. I may regret this later, but my mouth is already moving.

"Um, Ms. Anita. Since Grandpa's almost all packed up, we're probably going to grab pizza tonight instead of cooking. Would you like to join us?"

Her face brightens in delight. "How lovely! Have your mother call me with the details. I have a Dames for Driftwood emergency luncheon that could go all afternoon."

That's the group from the council meeting. "Dames for Driftwood, hmm? What exactly do they do?"

"Oh, a little bit of everything. Book drives, beach cleanups," she says with a wave. "Today, they're collecting signatures for a measure to pause all zoning approvals. The town needs to study the impact of these new projects first. There's even chatter about recalling the council president for corruption. Apparently I missed quite the rousing council meeting the other day, and the Dames aren't the only ones fired up."

Ms. Anita waggles her eyebrows as if she knows how Leo and I were involved. She seems to consider our participation a good thing, though for reasons slightly different than my parents'.

My eyes widen. I may not have succeeded in saving Warner Place, but there's hope for the soul of Sunnyside after all.

"So should we save you a slice at dinner?" I ask.

"Why, of course. It's a date!"

I cringe at the word *date*. I brought this on myself, I know. I'll have to sit through her and Grandpa flirting, but I can at least make sure I sit at the far end of the table.

Soon, Mom and Dad exit the house, locking the door behind them one last time. We pile into the minivan, and Dad sets his GPS app for Grandpa's place, despite having driven there every day for the past two weeks. I mention Ms. Anita is joining us for dinner, and Mom does a quick search online for the best local pizza places.

We drive down Main Street, past the stores with beach decor, past Culpepper's Creamery, past the Cormorant Café. We stop at a red light, next to the old movie theater with the weathered marquee and faded paint. A woman wipes the dusty window of the ticket stand, and Dad stretches to see the words on the sign.

"Oh, look, there's a movie showing, if we want to catch that after dinner."

"What movie?" I ask.

"*Ghostbusters.*"

The light turns green, and we speed away in our van, Mom and Dad with zero clue as to why Leo and I are laughing.

ACKNOWLEDGMENTS

First, thank you to my agent, Natalie Lakosil, for being such a great advocate and sounding board. I'm proud to be part of the Looking Glass Literary family you've built.

To my wonderful editor, Amy Cloud, thank you for continuing to believe in me and my work. It's almost supernatural the way you're able to bring out what a story needs to make it shine. My thanks to the entire Storytide team as well, including Briana Wood, Andrea Vandergrift, and Lauren Dimaya for your beautiful art.

Thank you to Alechia Dow, Brittney Arena, Rae Castor, Alyssa Colman, Koren Enright, Sam Farkas, Jenn Gruenke, Jessica James, and Kalyn Josephson for inspiring me every day with your own phenomenal work and strength. Thank you also to Traci Adair, Jennifer Franz, Brittani Miller, and Horse for the emotional and metaphysical support. Rossini Yen, your middle-of-the-night messages lovingly and hilariously remind me there's more to us as people than our work. Chris and Jess Ford, workshopping the book title with you over tacos is a major highlight of my writing career.

To Emily Lloyd-Jones, Linsey Miller, Rosiee Thor, and Kalyn, my roomies in the vacation rental with the writing-miracle plumbing: it was such a gift to share a space with you, bask in your creativity, and eat all the bread.

To the Fuzzy Jackets crew, Kat De Los Reyes, Andrella Gonzalez, Jonah Toleno, and Pauline Villanueva: thank you for so graciously dealing with my random panic texts and requests for delicious food.

My thanks to my FALSD, NFALA, Pinay Powerhouse, and FYLPRO friends far and wide. I'm blessed to find myself surrounded by such amazing, accomplished people. Shout-out to Nikki Chan for the best book-dog name ever!

Thank you also to the entire San Diego Fiction Authors group for so much in-person joy and inspiration. Having you to celebrate and commiserate with is the best.

As with everything, all my gratitude to my family. Thank you to Mom, Dad, Reggie, Grandma, and Lalitha for your love, support, and cheerleading. Ruby and Raja, you two are the biggest reasons I do anything these days. Thank you for being your curious, loving selves. And finally, thank you to my husband, Rahul, for always pushing me to follow my heart and reminding me to rest.